Love Me A Little

By
Avery Easton

This is a work of fiction. Names, characters, places and events described herein are products of the author's imagination or are used fictitiously and are not to be construed as real. Any resemblance to actual events, locations, organizations, or persons, living or dead, is entirely coincidental.

ISBN 978-0-578-74719-4

Also available in eBook by Uncial Press, an imprint of GCT, Inc. Visit us at uncialpress.com

For Michael, my forever.

If you would like to enjoy the playlist that accompanies this novel, please search for *Love Me A Little* on your favorite music streaming site.

Spotify
Amazon
YouTube
Apple Music

Ethan Carter Returns to Lowenstein's

Jerome Miller chats with Broadway's favorite leading man in an exclusive interview with BroadwayChat.com.

Ethan Carter cuts a tall, slim figure in the doorway of the Brooklyn coffee shop where we meet to chat about his career and life. Two weeks from today, he hits the famed Lowenstein's stage. It's been five years since he last charmed us all on that stage—the live album is available on iTunes!--and his avid fan base, including yours truly, is eager to see him there again.

But don't try to get tickets for this one! It's already sold out. Shed no tears, though: according to Carter's publicist, he has shows lined up all up and down the East Coast where you can see the affable, genuine goofball up close and personal. We here at Broadway Chat sincerely hope his next project is a return to the Broadway stage!

Last seen three years ago in *What's Next*, for which he received a Tony nomination for originating the role of Hammond Smith, Carter has been absent from Broadway for too long. And we're ready to get him back. Carter graduated from Tisch School of the Arts twelve years ago, and his story from novice to star is one of ease. He was immediately scooped into a national tour, was the replacement Prince Charming in *Cinderella*, and that led to three more shows until he originated Hammond. It's easy to see how. He stands six-one, has a mop of messy sandy blonde hair, the brightest blue eyes, and a tenor that will touch the very core of your soul.

The lines around his eyes are a little more prominent since that first show, and at thirty-four, Carter opens up about his career, his life, and what's in store for him next.

JM: It's so exciting to see you going back to Lowenstein's. I can't wait to see the show!

EC: Thank you! I'm really excited to get back on that stage. I've been doing these big shows in concert halls and House of Blues type places. It's been fun feeling like a rock star, especially since I'm singing showtunes. But I'm excited to get a little more intimate with the audience here.

JM: What made you want to tour? You've had quite a bit of success lately, not just on the stage. Guest spots, film, a network show…

EC: That's true, and I'm really grateful. It's been mildly tumultuous lately. *Supersede* getting cancelled was a blow for sure. I wish that had gotten another season.

JM: I was sorry to hear it. I really loved that show. Spy dramas are so my thing.

EC: Thank you. But it's been fun these past few years, exploring that side of the business. I've been really lucky to get a lot of work. But performing in front of a live audience is where I'm really at home.

2

JM: And we loved you in the live TV version of *Company*. You were an incredible Bobby.

EC: Sondheim is a genius. I mean, I just fully revere him. Getting to be stripped that bare is hard enough on a stage with an audience, but doing it in front of millions on TV? That was such an incredible, unique experience. I will never forget that as long as I live.

JM: It seems like you could really relate to Bobby with where you are now in your life. Is that correct?

EC: Bobby's revelation in "Being Alive", when he finally realizes that being alone is not all it's cracked up to be, that hit me hard. I'm not sure how much acting I was doing in that moment, to be honest. I've been working so much and haven't had a lot of time to think about it. Now that all I'm doing is touring this show, I'm spending more time alone. And I'm starting to realize that…I'm open. "I'm ready now," as Bobby would say.

JM: Ladies…he's single!

Ethan just smirks at me and I know that's as far as I will get into his love life. He's an intensely private person, only talking about his work. You won't find much of his personal life on social media. Perhaps that's why his fans are so intense. The mystery of who Ethan Carter really is remains just that.

JM: You would certainly have your pick of fans. Your fanbase is something to behold. They are so loyal to you in every way. What do you think about being so universally adored?

EC: (*chuckling*) I'm really lucky. I have some really great, supportive fans out there, and I just want to continue to work and make them proud.

JM: They also lovingly refer to you as a complete--let me check my notes--dork.

EC: *(now laughing out loud)* They're not wrong! I'm a Grade-A nerd. When I was a kid, my mom would play classic Broadway cast recordings. I would get bullied because I ran around singing showtunes on the playground. I was lucky that my parents recognized that I had a little talent and steered me toward theatre. And now, I would rather stay in and read a biography of some long dead politician than go out these days. I love fantasy like *Game of Thrones* and *Lord of the Rings*. But I think the nerdiest thing about me is bowling. I'm really into bowling.

JM: That is unique, to say the least. And I don't know if nerdy is the word. Dorky dad, maybe?

EC: Definitely dorky dad. My dad and I have bowled together since I was a little kid. It's our bonding time. And I'm really good! My average is around 200. I've liked other sports--I ran track in high school and I played a little baseball, I still like basketball. But from a very young age, I was clearly a performer. I was always encouraged to pursue what interested me and not go with the mainstream. So being called a dork does not bother me. It's a badge I wear with pride.

JM: It also helps that you look like a Disney prince.

EC: I don't know about that. But thank you.

JM: Tell me more about the Lowenstein's show--I know it's going to be a deviation from the rest of your tour. What do you think your audience will make of it?

EC: I'm going to invite them to play a lot. That's the best part about Lowenstein's, everyone is sitting right there at tables in front of me. It's very intimate. There's no more fun

4

than engaging with people on that level. I hope everyone has a great time.

JM: So, what do you think is next for you? In your career *and* love?

EC: (*laughs again*) Come on, man. I'm not sure. I am continuing to do these shows. We're looking at Chicago and the West Coast as well. But as far as my next role, be it onstage or on film… I'll keep auditioning. And we'll see what happens.

Ethan Carter is humble, grateful, and one of the hardest workers I know in this business. Whatever he does next, he is sure to shine. Check out ethancarter.com/tour for dates and tickets.

CHAPTER ONE ♫

The lights from the city winked through the curtains of the rented Upper East Side condo, reflecting off the gleaming surfaces of the open living area. A surge of emotion flowed through Evie. She tucked a strand of hair behind her ear; the rest fell in waves cascading down her back. She breathed deeply and closed her eyes, allowing the excitement to overtake her. Daniel appeared behind her in the full-length mirror, adjusting his bow tie.

"Ethan Carter," she breathed, "right in front of us, close enough to touch. I can't believe it!"

"And I can't believe how wonderful it is to see you so excited," Daniel said.

Evie grinned at him, surprising herself at the glee she felt. She bent down to tie her Chuck Taylors, which she wore with a little black dress. Two rings hung from the chain around her neck, and she tucked it neatly into her dress. She ran a hand through her hair and looked at herself in the full-length mirror. She smiled to herself when she saw how her eyes sparkled in anticipation.

"I'll never get you in heels, will I?" Daniel asked from behind her.

"Heels are a construct of the patriarchy and they were worn by men first..." She clapped her hand over her mouth. *Damn, there I go again.*

"I know, I know, I'm teasing." Her lecture on high heels had been a running joke during their ten-year-long friendship. "You look marvelous, my darling."

"You know what?" she said, "I *feel* marvelous. And I think you were right. I think Ethan *is* going to notice." She shimmied her shoulders a little in the mirror.

Daniel chuckled and kissed the top of her head. "I missed this. And as happy as I am to hear you talk about flirting, don't you think he'll be too busy singing to notice anyone in the audience?"

She rolled her eyes. "Are you really trying to take away the first time I feel pretty in forever?"

A smile spread across Daniel's face. "You always look pretty."

"Twenty bucks says he flirts with me," Evie said as their eyes met in the mirror. She lifted her chin stubbornly, feeling a confidence she hadn't felt for over a year.

"Oh, that's a bet I will definitely take," he said. She knew by his teasing tone that he was pleased this silly banter was back.

They shook hands, gathered their things, and walked out the door together.

§

Ethan Carter set down his phone after reading through Jerome Miller's piece again, thinking what he always thought about his interviews, that he came off a little vapid. But he played everything close to the vest on purpose. He supposed he'd rather play a little dumb than have his entire emotional state on the internet for the world to see.

He examined his eyes in the dressing room mirror. The lines around them were a little more prominent, as Jerome had pointed out. But he didn't mind. He felt they represented all the growth and all the lessons he'd learned through his twenties until now, nearly halfway through his thirties.

He kept mentally playing back the part of the interview which Jerome had told him could be off the record. He had even turned off his recorder. And he'd asked about Paige. Since Ethan and Jerome had been friends since the early days, Ethan had been completely comfortable telling him what had happened...

His ex, Paige, was beautiful, energetic, and fun to be around when she wasn't needling him about their relationship. His strictness about his private life rankled her far more than it should. She'd wanted him to go public about their relationship after just a few months.

He didn't have the heart to tell her that the reason he didn't want to put her in the spotlight was because he knew she wasn't the *one*. That, and her penchant for posting about every inside joke, every dinner out, every little fight. Nothing was too small to passive-aggressively Tweet about.

He tried to keep it under wraps, but rumors still spread. At least they were true. And he was always somehow able to let rumors--be they about his sexuality, his work, or his love life--roll right off his back. He supposed that after a year, off and on, Paige deserved more from him than he was able to give. He should have been more careful with her heart.

The breakup had been two months ago, and he still couldn't shake what he'd said to her the last time they spoke. After a week of ignoring his texts and calls, during which Ethan felt more and more desperate to see her, Paige showed up at his apartment one Thursday night.

She'd finally scored a chorus role in a Broadway show and thus her ego knew no bounds. She told him that he was getting everything he wanted, that they were becoming Broadway's power couple. He had gaped at her, disbelieving a person could be so manipulative and know

8

him so little after a year. Finally, he saw her for what she was, a social climber with a desperate insecurity.

But then she had walked slowly towards him, slipping the straps of her sundress down her shoulders. She'd let the dress pool on the floor, and he recognized she was wearing his favorite set of lingerie. He reached for her as if on autopilot and she had taken the cue. She'd kissed him. Hating himself a little, he'd given in. She was a tiger in bed after all, and sex had always been the best part of their relationship.

Afterwards, she had left his head buzzing as she always did.

She trailed her fingers on his chest. "I'm so excited you changed your mind. I can't wait to walk the red carpet with you. Opening nights, movie premieres, the Tonys..."

That was it, the impetus he needed to completely lose it. A week of not hearing from her, all the manipulation, the total disrespect of his wishes, everything came to a head. He'd leapt out of bed and yanked on his underwear.

"I've made myself very clear!" he yelled. "You're *not* the one for me, I'm *not* going public about you, and you're a fucking crazy *bitch*!"

He wasn't so proud of that last part. He winced a little at the memory and took a deep breath. He had never called a woman a bitch to her face before, and he still hated himself for it.

Paige had screamed at him, crying as she dressed. She called him a self-absorbed, rich kid asshole with nothing of substance to himself, a shallow nobody who loves to show off.

He'd closed--well, slammed--the door on her and breathed a sigh of relief, while trying to remember how she'd gotten so under his skin in the first place. He tried so hard to be a good person, and she knew exactly what to say to hurt him. The names she'd called him stung the most. The next week brought him a storm of angry texts and voicemails. As a result, he'd chalked up the last year of his life with Paige to great sex, a few laughs, and at least some entertaining drama.

Jerome gaped at him after hearing this story. "Yikes, my friend. That isn't what I expected to hear."

"It wasn't my proudest moment," Ethan said.

Jerome just nodded and turned the recorder back on...

Ethan grimaced in the mirror at the memories. He checked the time on his phone. A photo of Henry, his part-Labrador mutt, greeted him on the homescreen. He smiled. Getting a dog to offset the loneliness had been his best idea, possibly ever. Especially since Paige had started texting and Tweeting at him again.

He sighed and stared at his reflection again. *I'm ready now.* His heart was open, but it was difficult to know who to trust. He was waiting for that spark, what his married friends told him was almost instantaneous.

His mind turned to his fans as he tried to tame his mop of hair. While still a niche celebrity--the paparazzi didn't chase him down and he could usually walk down the street without being recognized--he had admirers all over the globe. Musical theatre fans are notoriously obsessive, and he had also managed to work on films and television shows with cult-like followings. Even the smallest role in an independent film was enough for fans on social media to obsess over him. They were fun for an ego boost, but he couldn't possibly date one of them. Not to mention that with all the traveling and working he'd been doing, he didn't have much time to devote to someone anyway. And yet.

He wasn't afraid to admit he was a bit lonely.

"Three minutes, Mr. Carter," Max, his stage manager and one of his closest friends, said from his dressing room doorway.

Ethan shook his head clear of his reverie. "Thanks, man." He inhaled and exhaled deeply, trilled his lips a few times, and took one more gulp of honeyed tea. His hands were sweating. That was unusual. Nerves didn't always get him, but when they did, this is how it started. Something was in the air tonight.

"Hey," he said, "do a shot with me."

Max smiled wide and tucked his headset around his neck. "Anything for you, boss."

Ethan pulled a flask from his messenger bag and poured two shots into the paper cups usually reserved for mouthwash.

Max raised his cup. "To life. And a good show."

"L'chaim," Ethan said, and they threw back the Buffalo Trace.

A tinny voice came from the headset and Max tipped his head towards it. "Hey, that's a one-minute warning, Mr. Carter."

Ethan chuckled and took another sip of tea. "Thank you, one," he said, "and quit calling me mister." He punched Max's shoulder, pulled on his suit jacket, and followed Max down the hallway and up the stairs.

He could hear the crowd as the plates were being cleared and second or third drinks were ordered. Hopping a little on the balls of his feet while he stretched and breathed, Ethan closed his eyes and said a silent prayer to whomever that tonight would go well.

The band started a little intro music and silence fell. Ethan heard himself being announced. He smiled widely, opened his eyes, and walked onto the stage and into his spotlight. Before him, an enthusiastic crowd was on their feet. He could just make out the beautiful old venue. Though its striped wallpaper was fading, and the floor could stand replacing, it was still the dream of every Broadway performer to stand where he was standing: where legends had once stood. The front of the stage jutted into the surrounding cabaret tables. His band played beneath his introductory hello and some banter with his audience. After a minute or two, he began to sing.

As he sang and saw the smiles on his audience's faces, his nerves began to subside. This was where he belonged. He noticed a tall man and a red-haired woman at one of the front cabaret tables. The redhead had a huge laugh and a bright smile, which he appreciated. He usually chose a suburban mom to play to in venues like this, but this girl was hard to resist. Plus, she would be a perfect player in his next song.

"So, this next song is one of my favorites. It's about a young man with a crush on a beautiful Irish girl," he said into the mic. The band started his intro, and Ethan looked directly at the redhead.

Her eyes sparkled back at him, inviting and warm.

As he sang, he walked off the stage and into the audience. He flirted with a couple of older women as he made his way to the redhead and her date. She played right along, eyes dancing, laughing in all the right places. Ethan took her hand as he sang, noticing the freckles on her shoulders and the bridge of her nose. Though he almost exclusively dated brunettes, he was a sucker for redheads. This woman was no exception.

The song swung to the end. As he backed away up to the stage, he noticed that with her simple black dress, she wore Chucks identical to the ones in his bag backstage. A little thrill ran through him as the song ended and he thanked everyone for playing along.

Emboldened by the shot and the freckles, he said to the redhead, "So was that our first date, basically?"

She threw her head back, laughing with abandon. "Maybe. Do you want it to be?"

"Maybe. What's your name?"

A pause, before she said, "A girl has no name." Her expression remained stoic, but her eyes laughed.

Ethan gaped. *Gorgeous, and she banters.* "Did you just reference *Game of Thrones* at me?"

She just laughed, shrugging.

"Should we just get married?"

She faltered for an almost indiscernible second, then smiled, saying, "Are you proposing?"

Okay, she gave as well as she got, and he had to move on. He winked at her.

"We'll see, Arya. This next song…"

As the show continued, Ethan kept catching the redhead's eye. She was a great audience, engaged, laughing out loud in all the right places, clapping enthusiastically. After an encore of "Do I Love You" from *Cinderella*, Ethan triumphantly headed backstage.

Max was waiting for him. "You love her," he said, grinning ear to ear.

"Shut up."

"I'll do no such thing."

"She was fun to play off of...actually..."

"Uh huh..."

"Have her come back so I can thank her? And apologize for flirting with her in front of her date?" Ethan said casually. Max's grin widened.

"You're transparent, dude. I'm on it." He clapped Ethan on the shoulder and disappeared. Ethan shook his head and went to the green room where a few friends and his band were waiting. Amid congratulations he kept his eye on the door, wondering who the hell the girl was, and why he felt so affected by her.

CHAPTER TWO ♫

Evie smiled at Daniel and held out her hand.

He glared while reaching into his wallet and slapped a twenty-dollar bill into her waiting palm.

"Told ya," she gloated.

"Unbelievable."

"It's the hair."

"And the bedroom eyes, you minx."

"Those helped, too."

Daniel glanced around. "I honestly don't think we should leave out the front door. You might get jumped."

Evie looked around the room at Ethan's fans, some of whom were eyeing her with malice. "Holy shit, the glaring."

"*I'm* even getting glared at," Daniel said, sounding surprised and delighted.

"The proximity to awesomeness and the hand that Ethan touched could be very dangerous for you." Evie held her hand out regally. Daniel chuckled and kissed it.

"Is there a back way out? Or could we have another drink before we leave?" he said.

"You don't honestly think anyone would come at us, do you?" Evie said.

"No, but I love the idea of all that drama," Daniel said.

Evie rolled her eyes. "Fine, let's see if there's a back way out...or more whiskey." She stood and so did Daniel, after straightening his bow tie.

A young man in black and wearing a headset approached them. "Excuse me, miss?"

Daniel smiled widely at him, as if sizing him up. "Hello," he drawled, "I'm Daniel, how can we help you?"

Evie rolled her eyes again, grinning at Daniel's ability to flirt with literally anyone. "Hi, what's up?"

"Mr. Carter would like to meet you backstage and thank you for playing along tonight. If you'll come with me."

"What? Whoa. That's so sweet, but he really doesn't have to do that..." Evie said.

"No, he really does, come on, come with me," he said, and offered his arm.

She set down her drink. "Listen, it's really kind of him to ask us to come back, and I love that I won the Ethan-will-flirt-with-Evie bet, but truly, he can enjoy his night. He doesn't have to do that."

The young man dropped his professional demeanor so quickly it was almost funny. He seemed startled that a fan would say no to meeting Ethan Carter.

"Girl, listen. Ethan doesn't do this basically ever, and I really want to tell him I had to convince you. He's getting a little too big for his britches, if you ask me. I'm Max, by the way."

Daniel and Evie both laughed and shook his hand.

"Okay, okay, but only for you, Max. It's very nice of him to ask."

Max proffered his arm again, but this time Daniel took it.

"Now, Max, was it? You're the stage manager? Fascinating, tell me literally everything about that," Daniel said as they headed backstage.

Evie watched them go for a moment, amused. She drained the rest of her Buffalo Trace and followed behind them to the stairwell.

§

"Oh really, just for his shows? Do you act, too?" Ethan heard a man say from the hall. He was leaning against the makeup counter in the green room, listening to the idle chatter and sipping water. He heard Max's answer, something about not really loving the spotlight, and grinned to himself. Max and the guy from the front table walked into the room. Max gave Ethan a nod and a huge grin. They took a seat on the small couch as Ethan turned to the door.

The redhead was there, examining her surroundings with a keen eye. With a laugh as big as hers, she was shorter than he expected. When her gaze landed on his, she smiled widely. "You wanted to see me, Mr. Carter?"

That little thrill ran through him again as she walked towards him, totally at ease. "Yeah, thank you so much for coming down. I just wanted to thank you for being such a great sport tonight. Going into the audience is always risky, and you made it worth the while." He opened his arms and she stepped into them without hesitation. To his surprise the hug felt exactly right, as if she belonged in his arms.

"Ha! Well good, I'm glad I could help," she said, and pulled away. "You actually settled a bet, so thanks for the twenty bucks." She slid onto the makeup counter, making herself comfortable.

"Really, what bet was that?" he said, stepping closer.

"That you'd flirt with me."

Ethan gasped and put a hand over his heart, pretending to be affronted. "I did no such thing. I'm an *ac-tor*!" He flourished his arms dramatically.

Evie laughed. "Well, real or fake, I'm all the richer for it. So, thanks." She paused. "Getting away to hear a pretty man sing pretty things was exactly what I needed tonight."

"Well, happy to oblige in both ways, then," Ethan said.

They smiled at each other, probably holding the gaze longer than necessary.

After a moment she frowned, but her eyes were alight. "Good lord man, you're like staring into the sun. How is it possible that you are that handsome?"

He blinked at the compliment, not that he wasn't used to it, but she was so genuine that it threw him. "You don't mince words, do you? And have *you* looked in a mirror lately, Freckles?"

"Life is too short to mince," she said softly. She hopped off the counter. "Thank you for asking us back here. I've been a great admirer for a long time, and we had a blast tonight. Your talent is ridiculous, and your voice is just…breathtaking." She held out her hand.

He glanced at it, not willing to let the encounter go just yet. "So, do you have a name or not?" He grinned but didn't accept her hand.

She dropped it. "I am no one."

Once again, she had referred to *Game of Thrones*. "Okay, you don't want me to know." He rolled his eyes, pretending to be offended.

"It's Evelyn. Evie."

"That's really pretty."

"I was named after my grandmother, who was basically the baddest bitch that ever lived."

Ethan realized that they were much closer to each other than before, with an unexplained heat passing between them. Who was this girl, and what was this invisible pull she had on him?

"I come from a long line of baddest bitches, so that's pretty awesome." Ethan held her gaze for several beats and was aware that his breathing had deepened. If he wasn't mistaken, so had hers.

As they continued chatting, she kept complimenting him, the kind words seeming to fall out of her mouth. It was hard for him to ignore the energy between them. It seemed to him that she felt it too.

17

"Well," she said finally, "we should get out of your hair and let you enjoy the rest of your night."

"That's what we were thinking." Ethan's drummer shook his hand. The rest of the band said goodnight and followed the drummer out the door. Soon, the only others left in the room were Max and Daniel. Ethan nudged Evie, nodding at them. They were deep in conversation on the couch. He cleared his throat. Daniel startled at the sound. Both he and Max seemed to suddenly realize the room had emptied.

"Oh, hi, guys." Max caught Ethan's eye and grinned sheepishly. Daniel stood, chuckling a little.

"We weren't properly introduced. I'm Daniel."

Ethan shook his outstretched hand. "Nice to meet you. Thank you so much for coming."

"My pleasure. Your pianist was really something. Not everyone can handle Jason Robert Brown's rhythms like that."

"She's incredible, isn't she? I got lucky when she agreed to play for me." The four of them chatted a few minutes more. Ethan was hyperaware of Evie's presence next to him.

"So," she said when a natural silence fell, "We really should let you get back to your night. Thanks for everything. You're…just as real as you seem."

It was exactly how Ethan wanted every fan to feel. "That's really good to hear," he said. There was another long beat as Ethan held her gaze.

"Do you want to come with us for a drink? I'm too keyed up to go home," he finally blurted. He felt ridiculous immediately, knowing what his publicist would say to him inviting a fan out for a drink. But there was something different about both Evie and Daniel. Both felt like friends already. *And you're a grown ass man, you can do what you want.*

Evie bit her lower lip and glanced at Daniel. "Yeah, okay, sure," she said hesitantly.

Ethan crowed, "A ringing endorsement." But he noted a change in her, as if a light had gone out.

Daniel stepped towards Evie and put his arm around her. "Gentlemen, we graciously accept your kind invitation. We'd love to join you." He was smiling widely.

Evie was standing very still.

"I'm just-- Is there a bathroom down here?" She sounded a little breathless.

Ethan told her where the bathroom was and she touched his forearm on her way out, causing the thrill down his spine again.

Ethan watched Evie go and turned to Daniel, who said, "She's a magnet, isn't she?"

"She really is. What's uh...what's her...is she..." Ethan shut his mouth and brought a hand to the back of his neck.

"What Evie is, is thirty-three, she's fun, hilarious, and whip smart. The rest is her story," Daniel said.

Ethan hesitated but before he could ask another question, Daniel continued.

"Oh. Also, yes, she's single. God, you really are transparent. Max is right."

"Max? Come on!"

Max just blinked innocently. "Well, come on. If one of the oldies had played with you like that, you never would have asked her backstage."

"True as that may be, loyalty, Max, jeez." Ethan pouted.

Daniel laughed. "Don't worry, friend, your secret is safe with me. She's one of the best people on Earth. I get it."

Ethan remembered the little thrill when he saw her in the audience, when she came into the room, when she touched his arm. He supposed she was one of those women, the kind who brought light to wherever she went. There was something special about her, and he wanted to know more.

§

In the small bathroom, Evie forced herself to stand still, close her eyes, and breathe. Eventually she calmed and looked into the mirror. She reached into her dress and pulled up her necklace. Palming the two rings, she whispered, "Move on, be happy."

§

"My ears are burning," Evie said, when she sauntered back into the green room.

Ethan beamed at her. "I'll grab my bag and we can go out the back." He started toward his dressing room. This time, he trailed his hand down Evie's arm as he passed.

Evie knew her shudder was visible when Ethan touched her in passing. "Jesus, is he serious with the animal magnetism? My god," she said when he'd left.

Max, who'd pulled a button-down shirt out of a bag, grinned. "It's crazy, isn't it?" he said as he slipped the shirt on over his black tee. "And he's incredibly kind and funny and down-to-earth. We've been friends since high school and he's never once been an egomaniac with me."

Evie mulled over Max's thoughtfulness as he led them out to the stage door. She was impressed that someone like Ethan had maintained a high school friendship even after everything he had accomplished.

Only a few fans lingered at the stage door. When Ethan's car pulled up, Max ushered Evie and Daniel inside. Ethan came out quickly and got in the back door, waving to his fans from the window. Max took the front seat, beside the driver.

Evie's thigh pressed against Ethan's in the cramped space. She shivered again.

The bar near the Brooklyn Bridge was exactly the kind of bar Evie liked: a divey joint with no tourists. This was exactly the kind of night life she was interested in.

It wasn't quite ten, so there was still a table open, and the four new friends settled in after ordering drinks. When Daniel and Max started to debate the merits of clubs versus dive bars, Ethan turned to Evie. "So, do you live in Manhattan?"

"Actually no. I'm in Chicago. For the last twelve years," she said.

Ethan was visibly saddened by the news. "I like Chicago. Too bad you don't live here though." He sipped his whiskey, while eyeing her.

Evie arched an eyebrow, not quite believing that Ethan Carter was so blatantly hitting on her. "Oh really? Well, I'm here until Tuesday, anyway."

"What brings you here?"

"Seriously? Your show, dummy. Besides, I like it here. And Daniel's auditions. He's going in for a new musical and he's also in the running to replace Gunner Collins in *Fully Engaged*. If they go well, I'll be here a lot."

"Oh yeah, I heard Gunner was leaving the show. And what made you want to see my cabaret?"

Evie gaped. "Are you being purposefully obtuse and digging for compliments?" She swatted him on the arm.

He pretended to wince. "Absolutely, yes."

"Well, as long as we're being honest," she snickered. "Like I said, I've admired you for years. Your voice is unbelievable. I loved all your films and TV shows, and you've always been so genuine in all your press. I wanted to see if you were the real deal."

"Oh? And am I?" He leaned closer so they could hear each other over the din.

Evie looked into his eyes. "I'm happy to report that you are." They regarded each other for a moment.

"How are you single?" There was a smile pulling at his lips.

Evie pulled back a little. "How do you even know that?" she said, baffled.

"Daniel told me. I was fishing."

"You're really not afraid to go after what you want, are you?"

"Nope. And I don't think you are either."

Evie regarded him for a few moments before answering his question. "We're being honest tonight, right?"

"Tonight, and always."

"Okay, but you have to promise not to make the face," she said, and set down her drink.

"The face?" He sounded mystified.

"Just promise."

He hooked his pinky finger into hers. "I won't make whatever face you are talking about. I promise."

The prolonged contact made her heart beat faster.

"Okay. My husband..." Evie took a deep breath. "He... Well, he died. Okay? A little over a year ago. Don't make the face!"

But she was too late. Ethan's expression had fallen into one of sympathy and pity.

"I'm so sorry."

"Why? Did *you* kill him?"

CHAPTER THREE ♫

One Year Ago, July

The wind whipped past Evie's and Liam's faces, and the craggy villages rose before them as the boat flew along the lake. She gazed at the beauty of Lake Como, as she tried to trap her flying hair with a hair tie. Liam uncorked a bottle of champagne, poured two glasses, and handed one to her. His smile brightened as he toasted her. She smiled back and drank. The bubbles were festive, the sun was warm, and the O'Haras were content.

Wordlessly, they moved to the back of the small boat. Liam wrapped his arms around Evie, and she rested her back against his chest.

He kissed her neck. "Happy birthday, sweet thing," he murmured in her ear.

She closed her eyes and smiled. "Best birthday ever."

He put a hand to the side of her face and lowered his lips to hers. The kiss lingered and deepened. Evie pulled back a bit reluctantly. She didn't want to miss the view. "Can you believe this place?" Liam said wonderingly as he gestured at the mountains, the colorful villages flying by, the sun beginning to set.

"I really can't," Evie said, "and I'll say it again. Best. Birthday. Ever."

"Best *wife* ever." Liam pulled her closer.

"Best *husband* ever," she replied. She kissed him again, feeling a deep gratitude for him and all they had together.

Their vacation was almost impromptu. A friend of Liam's had decided to purchase a home on Lake Como in Italy and asked Liam to check it out with him. When Liam noticed the trip fell on Evie's birthday, they decided to make a vacation out of it. So here they were, enjoying a private boat ride at the end of a leisurely week filled with incredible food, the company of good friends, and some of the most amazing vistas either of them had ever seen.

When they'd met, Evie fell instantly in love with Liam, and he'd felt the same. Immediately, they intertwined their lives. It didn't take long for them to move in together, for Liam to propose, Evie to plan the wedding, and their lives together to begin. They dodged the kids question they were constantly asked by explaining their life was exactly how they wanted it. Both were passionate about their work and each other. They had a beautiful home in Chicago. While their marriage wasn't without its trials, it was a happy one.

"Seriously, I can't believe we are here. That this place even exists…what the hell. There is so much beauty I can't stand it," Evie said.

"We're very lucky people, aren't we?" Liam said.

She tipped her glass against his. "That we are, buddy, that we are."

Liam opened the picnic basket and brought out the nectarines, cheese, and crackers he had packed. The nectarines were still warm from where they'd picked them off the tree outside their villa window that afternoon. They ate, enjoying each other's easy company. Evie didn't want the boat ride to end, even though what awaited them later was a wonderful dinner up in the mountains.

She poured more champagne and gazed into her handsome husband's deep brown eyes. They twinkled at her with an intimacy that can only come from knowing every part of someone, the good and the bad and the in-between.

He tucked a strand of hair Evie hadn't managed to catch behind her ear. "I'm the luckiest man in the world, Evelyn O'Hara," he said. "I love you more than cookies."

She smiled at his words, his sweet tooth being a point of amusement in their marriage. "More than cake?"

"More than cake and brownies and even pie."

"Tall words, my friend," she said, and wrapped her arms around his neck. "I love you, too."

He kissed the tip of her nose. She moved in closer and her lips tenderly met his.

Interrupting their embrace, their driver turned around to point out an ancient Roman bridge they were passing.

At the same time another boat came speeding out of a nearby dock, directly toward them. Their driver swerved to avoid it.

Evie staggered with the abrupt movement. And suddenly, Liam was gone.

One Week Later

Only one memory remained from that next week. The rest was forever blank.

All she could remember was the sound of her own screams. They came to her from far away, as if she were hearing them from underwater.

She couldn't remember half laughing at the sight of her husband flying overboard, because what could happen? They'd fish him out and have a good laugh before heading back to their villa to change for dinner.

She couldn't remember the other boat swerving back to them, having seen someone go overboard.

She couldn't remember their driver stopping their boat and rushing to the side.

She couldn't remember the driver grasping Liam's lifeless arm, couldn't remember not understanding why Liam didn't try to pull himself out of the water.

She couldn't remember the gush of blood from Liam's temple. Or the attempts of the driver and the other boat's occupants to stop the bleeding, to perform CPR.

She couldn't remember the rush to land, the ambulance, the unfamiliar Italian hospital, the gentle doctor who held her hands, who told her in a lilting accent too beautiful for the words it delivered that her life was changed forever.

She couldn't remember the flight back to Chicago, which she only survived by taking the sleeping pills the doctor had given her.

All she could remember was the screaming.

Hers.

August

Liam's memorial was long over. Evie's refrigerator was overstocked with food she couldn't face eating. Friends and family had come and gone. Their concerned looks had begun to grate on her nerves. She couldn't stand them looking at her with such pity.

She needed solitude. She needed to retreat. She needed to remember and to forget. She'd thought her heart was safe. Forever.

The memories began to come back to Evie in patches. She remembered the Italian doctor's hands holding hers, remembered the wedding ring glinting on the doctor's left hand. It was almost ostentatious, a diamond the size of a small stone catching the hospital's fluorescent lights.

Evie didn't wear a diamond. She preferred her thin gold band and its simplicity.

She remembered--and tried to forget--Liam's body lying on the deck of the boat as strangers, speaking rapid Italian she couldn't understand, tried to revive him.

It came back to her eventually. That whole terrible day, that had started out so beautifully, hit her like a punch in her gut every time a new memory came back to her. When a check from the life insurance company was delivered, she emailed the educational theatre non-profit she worked for and took an indefinitely long leave of absence.

She retreated, leaving her phone unanswered, letting the numbers of texts she'd received mount. It didn't matter anymore.

Her world became smaller. She rarely left the bedroom she had shared with Liam, sleeping fourteen hours at a time, or sometimes not at all. She moved only to accept deliveries of essentials, certain she looked like a ghost to the delivery drivers. She kept the cat, Norman, fed, but instead of the regimented diet she'd had him on, she poured dry food liberally into his bowl. He grew plump. Norman was agitated, often pawing at Liam's pillow, as if wondering why he wasn't there indulging him in extra treats.

The door to the guest room, which had doubled as Liam's retreat, remained closed. Evie couldn't bring herself to look at all his guitars, his books, his video games. She'd closed the door and didn't open it again.

Every so often one of her neighbors would knock. When she opened the door, hours or days later, she would find a baked good with a sympathetic note attached.

She felt the loss of Liam to the very depths of her soul. Excepting one person, she could face no one.

Daniel was her only visitor. She merely tolerated him, only because he wouldn't give back her extra set of keys. After over a decade, she and Daniel had an intimacy of friendship that she didn't have with anyone else. They regarded each other as family. Before the accident, they had often joked that he was the real love of her life, a joke that seemed callous now.

Every other day or so, Daniel would arrive from his apartment down the street from her condo--hers now, hers alone--bringing news of their friends, of the Chicago Cubs season, of what theatre should be seen and what was getting bad reviews. He peppered the conversation with nonsense and gossip, as if hoping to ease some of Evie's pain for a few minutes.

He didn't talk about Liam, though she knew he grieved for him too. He just took care of Evie. Often, he would coax her into the shower, where she would give way to the tears that she wouldn't let come any other time. He would talk to her, even when she didn't or couldn't respond, would queue up mindless shows on Netflix, would make her meals, and he would hold her until she fell asleep. He had kept up with her family, from whom she had withdrawn, letting them know that he was getting her through it. Or trying.

It was the longest month Evie had ever spent. Every day seemed to stretch on for years. Each passing minute meant she was getting further away from her life with Liam, a concept she could barely fathom.

September

"Hello, my sunshine," Daniel called softly as he opened the door to Evie's condo. She stepped out of her bedroom in clean clothes, with her hair clean and shining. She could tell Daniel wanted to jump for joy, but he refrained. "Well my goodness, look at you," he said instead.

"Morning," Evie said, with a small, quick smile. She saw his eyes fill with tears. He rushed to her and hugged her tightly to him. "I thought you were never coming back," he said into her hair.

She put her arms around him. "I don't know that I'm...back...but...I did feel a little more like myself this morning," she said into his chest.

He squeezed her and pulled away, while looking down at her face. "Baby steps," he said, and pulled her in again.

Later that afternoon, after they'd done some binge watching, Daniel pulled a card from his wallet. He handed it to her. "I didn't want to give this to you too soon."

She regarded it skeptically.

"I think you should call Dr. Reichs. She's very highly recommended, and I think she'll be able to help you."

"Do I need help?" Evie asked in a small voice, meeting Daniel's eyes. He gestured to the usually meticulously clean bedroom which was now strewn with used tissues and unwashed glasses and plates, the detritus of grief. She followed his gaze around the room.

"What would *you* say to you?" he said.

For the first time in two months, Evie burst out laughing. "No fair using my logic on me," she said, and snuggled against Daniel's chest.

He chuckled and pressed play again.

October

Evie was starting to feel a little more herself again. Calling Dr. Reichs had been the right decision, especially as, shortly after her first session, Liam's remains finally arrived from Italy. The doctor prescribed medication to get her back to a place where she would want to leave her house again, but also acknowledged that her grief would be a long-term relationship that was in its earliest stages. She encouraged Evie to feel her feelings and to get out and help others.

Evie did. She began to volunteer for a women's shelter in her neighborhood and was content to lose herself in minding the front desk, organizing supplies from donations, and talking with the residents.

She also discovered Ethan Carter again. Once her favorite Broadway crush, she'd let her fantasies subside once Liam came along. She'd always been a music and theatre lover, could hold her own at karaoke, and had performed in many an amateur musical. She loved to sing along with Ethan's cast recordings. There was something incredibly charming about him--he seemed so sweet and had such a genuine smile.

One day, like a flash out of the blue, Evie had remembered his live album from a Lowenstein's show he'd done years before. She'd pulled the album up on her phone. It was the first music she had listened to in months.

And oh, that voice.

Ethan's voice was all at once sensual and comforting, smooth as butter. He sang a version of "Left Behind" from *Spring Awakening* and she shivered her way through it. His rendition of "Wishing You Were Somehow Here Again" from *The Phantom of the Opera*, modified for his beautiful tenor, sent tremors coursing through her and she cried for what felt like hours, playing the song on loop.

And she didn't even particularly like Andrew Lloyd Weber.

All this while, life without Liam was slowly becoming a reality.

He wasn't coming home.

February

"Are you sure you're up for this?" Daniel asked Evie as he helped her with her coat. Daniel, a sought-after Chicago stage actor, was opening a production at the Royal George, and tonight promised good vibes and champagne, exactly what they both needed.

She glanced at him incredulously. "Have I ever missed an opening night of yours?"

"Never, that's why we're still friends."

"Well then. Let's go." Evie headed for the door. She paused with her hand on the handle, thinking about the walks she had taken around her neighborhood. Anonymous in a hat and sunglasses, she'd walked for hours, listening to Ethan Carter sing about love and loss and happiness and hope. It was the most healing thing she was accomplishing at the moment. She was nervous about speaking to her friends and acquaintances tonight. She didn't want to be treated differently.

"And you'll be okay keeping an eye on me?" The uncertainty she felt was quite apparent in her voice.

"I will. I promise." Daniel paused. "Seriously, Eve, you don't have to come."

Feeling a forgotten strength from within herself, she turned and looked him in the eye.

"Danny," she paused, taking a deep breath, "I gotta get the fuck outta this house." With that, she whipped open the door. He laughed, and they tripped down the stairs. A giddiness overtook her as they hopped in a cab to go to the theatre.

After the show at the opening night reception, she could feel Daniel's eyes on her while he accepted his accolades. Though she usually loved to be the life of the party, she clung to the shadows, although she spoke to a few acquaintances and friends. Twice during the party, someone who didn't know asked about her husband. When she replied, Evie could hear an unintended sharpness in her voice. The two people who asked quickly but politely gave their condolences and walked away.

She took her leave early and promised Daniel that she would be able to get herself home.

April

Daniel had to all but shout over the music as he entered Evie's kitchen. "Are you seriously playing this again?"

She was cooking. Another improvement. Baby steps.

"You gonna mock a grieving widow's comfort music?" Evie pointed a spatula in Daniel's direction and raised her own voice to be heard over "Answer Me." "Ethan Carter's voice is… You know what? Shut up. It makes me happy and I'm not apologizing."

He brandished an envelope. "Well then, you will *love* this."

"Ooh, what is it? Gimme." She reached for it.

He pulled it away. "Let me preface this with: we are going to have a very difficult time come July. And we are going to get through it together. And after that, we're going to reward ourselves." He handed the envelope over.

Evie took it eagerly and ripped it open. She read the paper she pulled out and her eyes filled with tears.

Daniel was clearly shocked at her reaction. "What? No! No, this is happy. This is going to be happy."

Evie just shook her head. "You are the best friend in the entire world." She began to cry in earnest. "I don't know what I would have done without you for these past nine months. I don't think I would have made it. I--"

31

Daniel hugged her, and they crumpled to the floor. They cried together there, for minutes or hours. Who was counting?

Their tears dried eventually. The realization of what they were going to do dawned on Evie. He'd given her tickets to a front row table for Ethan Carter's long-awaited new cabaret at Lowenstein's in New York City.

"Holy shit, Danny, are we seriously going to be that close to him?" She looked down at the booking again.

He grinned widely. "Maybe I'll see if my agent can hook me up with some auditions while we're out there. See if I can get myself on Broadway."

"I'm sorry, do you think you're allowed to move to New York? Away from me?"

Daniel ignored her. "He's definitely going to flirt with you." He looked at her sideways, as if aware he was treading dangerous water.

Evie glanced at him and rolled her eyes. "Please. Nobody wants an old widow."

"You're thirty-two."

"Still."

"You're going to milk that old widow shit for all it's worth, aren't you?" he said, cautiously joking.

"Yes, the fuck I am." She was both surprised and relieved she could start joking about it.

"Here for it."

May

The medication Dr. Reichs prescribed dug Evie out of her serious depression. As she began to accept Liam was never coming back, she felt a bit more social.

At a birthday party for a friend, she fell into conversation with an old flame with whom she'd once had incredible chemistry. After a few glasses of wine and his sympathetic ear, she went home with him. He remembered the ways she loved to be touched, all at once familiar and new. But a nagging guilt kept her from hooking up with him again. Something felt off.

After talking with Dr. Reichs, she acknowledged that it had been too soon. But she agreed with the doctor that it was good she was opening up.

About the same time, Daniel's heart was broken by the violinist he was seeing. Evie took care of Daniel the way that he had been taking care of her. They commiserated. Daniel never once equated his breakup with her pain, and she never once diminished his pain over her own. Never had they been so happy to have each other. Evie found that taking care of Daniel had helped ease her denial and begin to move on.

The realization shocked her. But she decided survival is always shocking when it seems impossible.

July

Daniel was correct. The one-year anniversary of Liam's death was incredibly difficult, but Evie didn't want whatever he had planned. Her need to face this painful milestone in solitude was implicit.

On her birthday, which she would no longer acknowledge, she spent the day looking through photos, reading her journals, and remembering Liam in her own way. She cried for him and gathered him in her heart. She added her gold band to his ring on the chain around her neck, which she vowed not to remove.

In her session the next day, Dr. Reichs reminded her that it was okay to seek happiness, to move on. "Remember, Evie, everyone grieves on their own timeline. You are still young and deserving of love, and are allowed to find contentment, either alone or with someone else."

Evie clutched the rings as she listened. Yes, it was time to start letting life happen again.

Two weeks later, she and Daniel were in New York.

CHAPTER FOUR ♫

Ethan watched Evie's green eyes sparkle at him as they joked back and forth. As a naturally flirtatious person, bantering like this was pretty much his M.O., but the attraction he felt was giving it new weight. Her beauty drew him in, but it was her wittiness and confidence that sparked something else inside him. Greedily, he wanted to know everything about her.

"Okay, my husband…"

Except this. A divorce would not have surprised him, especially for someone his age. But…she was married? Daniel had lied? And why? *Why do I have such bad luck?*

"He… Well, he died. Okay? A little over a year ago. Don't make the face!"

But she was too late. He tilted his head to the side, his eyebrows knit together. "I'm so sorry."

"Why? Did *you* kill him?"

Flummoxed, Ethan stared. Her husband was dead. She was too young to feel such grief. He felt so sad for her, and he wanted to fold her in his arms, to comfort her, to tell her how sorry he was. Somehow, though, he could tell by the despondence in her eyes and the hard set of her mouth that saying any of that would push her away.

"Holy fuck..." he said before he could stop himself.

"Yep. We were on vacation in Lake Como, we were on a boat, it swerved, and he was tossed and hit his head. Instantly, I had no husband," Evie said. She snapped her fingers, as if she wanted to appear nonchalant. "Poof. Life changed forever."

"I literally have no other words than I'm sorry and holy fuck. That sucks," Ethan said.

Evie gave him a small smile. "Now why can't everyone use profanity to express their sympathy?" She laid a hand on his and gave it a squeeze. "Here's what, and this is all I'll say about it, because it's really no fun to talk about."

He squeezed back, letting her know she had the go-ahead.

"It was horrible. It was a garbage time in my life, and I truly felt like I was going to die. I spent months lying in bed, in our condo, barely taking care of our cat, and subsisting on crackers, basically. I had never felt so powerless, and for someone who had always felt pretty powerful, that was new. Daniel was indispensable." She nodded toward him. "He saved my life. He made me get up and shower and eat sometimes. He helped me call a psychiatrist, who put me on some medication to get me out of the hell I was in.

"After a few months, something clicked. I felt a sense of my old self returning and knew that I could either kill myself to be with him, or I could go on with my life."

"He wouldn't have wanted you to do that, though, right? Kill yourself?" Ethan interjected gently.

"Liam? Oh no, he definitely would have wanted me to Juliet myself immediately, rather than live without him." Evie chuckled.

Ethan joined in, pleased to hear her joke.

"Anyway, I decided to keep living, and here I am. It gets easier every day. And to answer your questions, yes, I still miss him. Yes, I'm moving on, and yes, he'll always be a part of me. The end."

Ethan realized that they were holding hands, her small ones in his large ones. He traced his thumb on her left ring finger. When she looked up at him, her eyes reflected a strength he knew was earned.

"That…is a super shitty story and I'm glad that you're alive," he said gently.

"And that is exactly how one should respond," Evie said, surprised at the ease with which she was discussing Liam's death. She found she could not break eye contact with Ethan.

Aware of a tightened tension buzzing in her chest, Evie said, "So, let me ask *you* a question, about your weird life."

"Please do."

"Your fans… They think you're this innocent, perfect guy. They idolize you as someone who can do no wrong. It's such a high pedestal they have you on. Does that just infuriate you? I mean, you're a thirty-four-year-old adult man. There's more to you than this goofy, sweet dude, who we all love of course, but…you have depth. That much is obvious. And I'm sure you have flaws. You definitely like bowling way too much."

Ethan snorted and raised his drink to his lips. "Honesty. Right?"

Evie nodded.

"And you're not a reporter? Because if you are this is off the record."

She snickered. "No, I am not a reporter. I'm not an anything anymore. I used to work for a theatre non-profit but… Dead husband, remember? Hefty life insurance policy."

Ethan raised his eyebrows and let out a short laugh.

"Good. You should laugh at morbidity. It's the only way to deal." She clinked her glass to his and took a drink.

"Okay. Then yes…it's fucking weird," he began. "Because I'm not perfect, and I'm not innocent. I *want* to be kind. I want to be genuine. And I am generally happy, and I feel really blessed to live my weird life. But all of that innocence nonsense makes me crazy. I suppose it's better than the alternative. I mean, I mess up, and I'm a little broken sometimes, and I can be a *huge* dick to girlfriends. In fact, the last one? I was an incredible asshole when we broke up. Definitely not one of my proudest moments."

"Was that around the Tonys?" Evie said.

Ethan looked startled. "How did you know that? There was nothing in the news or on social media."

Evie shrugged. "The light was out of your eyes. Smiles were a little forced. I'm not a creep, I'm just intuitive. I read people well. You're a great actor, but not a good pretender."

"Wow."

"Sorry."

"No. Wow, you're right. I'm not sure why I'm not creeped out right now, but I'm not." Their knees touched as they drew closer to each other.

Evie sat back and let a small, dangerous smile play on her lips. She took a sip of her whiskey. "Can I intuit something else?"

"Please. Read my mind."

"You're filthy in bed, aren't you, Carter?"

He put his hands on her knees and whispered into her ear, "Wouldn't you like to know?"

She inhaled sharply. "I should be so lucky."

He sat back, and they regarded each other once again. His gaze smoldered, confirming everything she knew about the importance of eye contact.

He shook his head. "I'm sorry," he said, breaking the delicious tension.

Evie blinked in surprise. "For?"

"You just lost your husband, and I'm all over you. I feel like an asshole."

Evie looked down at her drink. "Ethan…" she said, as she leaned towards him, "Mr. Carter. Do you think if I wasn't up for a flirt fest with my favorite Broadway star that

I would be here right now? Do I seem like the kind of person who would do anything she doesn't want to?"

"Not in the slightest." He sat forward so their faces were close once again.

"Good. I will tell you if I've reached some sort of limit."

He nodded. "Okay."

"Good. Continue," she said, and laid her hand on his knee.

He brushed her hair off her shoulder. "I've always been a sucker for freckles."

Evie felt good about what was happening with Ethan. Sparks were flying. This time, she didn't feel guilty or afraid, like she had after she slept with her old flame. Perhaps it was because there was no future here, or perhaps it was the whiskey impeding a better sense, but she'd be damned if he wasn't one of the sexiest human beings she had ever laid her eyes on. She wanted to spend as much time with him as he'd let her.

They ordered another round, and joined the conversation across the table. After a while, Max and Daniel shared a loaded glance and both began saying their goodnights. Evie watched Daniel go, and when he turned back at the door, she winked at him.

Once alone, Evie and Ethan playfully chatted some more. He wound a strand of her hair through his fingers and she didn't even try to stop herself from touching his arm or his thigh.

Finally, he said, "Do you want to go for a walk?"

Evie nodded wordlessly and they gathered their things. Outside on the sidewalk, Ethan gently took her hand. Something about the summer air eased the intensity of their flirtation, and she gazed up at him, her breath slowing. The amber glow of the streetlights softened his features.

Ethan traced her cheek with his finger, but he was frowning.

She shivered.

"Are you cold?" he said, without breaking eye contact.

"Nope."

Something had changed.

CHAPTER FIVE ♫

"Let's walk across the bridge."

She looked up at him, her surprise evident. "To Brooklyn?"

"Yeah."

"Okay."

As they walked, holding hands, Evie began to sing "The 59th Street Bridge Song" softly. She paused. "Huh. Making the morning last. I guess I finally understand what Paul and Art were talking about."

Ethan guffawed. He squeezed her hand, enjoying the sentiment, but he had to call her out. "Wrong bridge. And that was *ridiculously* cheesy."

"Guilty. I am prone to being a cheeseball."

His heart warmed as they ambled along, talking about their favorites and firsts, almost like a typical first date.

Evie stopped and turned around as they passed the halfway point of the bridge. She spent a few moments regarding the lights and the skyline. "Wow. This city is something special."

"And you live in *Chicago* for some reason."

"Hey, Chicago is amazing." Her playfulness returned, and they ribbed each other about their respective homes as they walked. They made it across the bridge to Brooklyn as midnight approached.

Ethan was buzzed and happy. Evie's hand in his felt so right. She made him laugh. Really laugh. As they talked about getting-to-know-you things--favorite books, movies, music, podcasts--he discovered how much they had in common.

Something was nudging the back of his mind, a new feeling of security, a new rhythm to a conversation. He tried to be objective, but it was getting harder the more he discovered about Evie.

"Can I intuit something else?" she said.

"Of course."

"You're a romantic."

"That's not intuition, I've literally said that a million times in interviews," he teased.

"Fair point. But you are one, yes?"

"I am. I like romance."

"Why?"

"Why do I like romance?" He considered for a few moments. "I don't know. It's a nice idea. Having someone to share things with and do things for. Someone to cook a meal for, and to send flowers just to see them smile, and like... I don't know... When something disappointing happens, having someone there to whine to and know they won't care if you're being unreasonable, or talk you down. Someone who'll give you perspective... Someone to touch, with actual feeling behind it..." As he spoke, he was aware of his thumb tracing her hand.

There was a pause as she appeared to digest his words. After a brief silence, she said, "That's not 'romance' per se. That's just...having a partner."

He looked over at her. "Do you miss that?"

He heard her inhale sharply as she stopped walking and her hand squeezed his. She was staring straight ahead.

"Limit," she said after a moment.

"Noted." He brought her hand to his lips, their fingers entwined, and kissed it.

She smiled tentatively up at him.

As they walked, the lights from a twenty-four hour bodega captured a man with a Great Dane on a leash. Laughter erupted around the corner and a group of kids dressed for clubbing crossed the street in front of them. Once they were gone, apart from a few cabs going by, this corner of the borough felt deserted.

Feeling bold, and without really considering the consequences, Ethan said, "So. Evie. Evelyn. Whose last name I don't even know. Do you like cheesecake?"

"Ooh, I do indeed." Evie answered.

He took her in his arms, dancing a waltz. It felt so natural. He spun her out and pulled her back, moving one hand to her waist, gently holding her other. She swayed with him, perfectly in sync.

"Are you a fan of *homemade* cheesecake?"

"The biggest."

"Well. My mother happens to make the most amazing cheesecake you will ever taste and--you're not even going to believe this--there is some in my apartment right now." He stopped swaying and gazed down at her. Her form fit perfectly against his. Ethan wasn't entirely certain this was a wise move, but then Evie smiled, and he felt completely assured that it was.

"Smooth," she said as she pulled away. "Very smooth."

He grinned and took her hand in his, holding his other arm out for a passing cab.

Once they were settled, she said, "O'Hara."

"Scarlett?" he said, puzzled.

"That's my last name. O'Hara."

"Evelyn O'Hara. Are you serious? Are you secretly a movie star from the forties?"

Throughout the short trip to his apartment, he attempted to impress upon her what a boon her name would be if she were an actor. She played along as he put on a Southern accent, adopting her own Georgia drawl.

They stepped out of the cab in front of his condo building, and he watched her look up at the modern structure, an inquisitive look on her face.

"So. Why do you live in Brooklyn? Shouldn't someone like you live near the theaters in Manhattan?"

He held the lobby door open for her. "Manhattan is pretty crowded, and I like the commute. Gives me time to think."

She stopped just outside the doorway, a half-smile on her face. "Hold up. How do I know you're not a serial killer?"

"Because I'm *super* famous and it would be tough to hide," he said, not even flinching at her mildly sarcastic question.

She pretended to consider, and then grinned. "Fair point. I'll trust you."

He grinned back and tried to usher her through, but she didn't move.

"Whoa, buddy, don't you want to ask me if *I'm* a serial killer?"

"Oh right, what was I thinking? *Are* you a serial killer?" He suppressed a chuckle and kept his face straight.

Evie narrowed her eyes and grinned that dangerous grin. "Not yet."

Ethan laughed. "Could you not start tonight? I have a meeting with my publicist tomorrow I really can't miss."

"Maybe," she teased, and they finally entered the building. The doorman waved to them and when the elevator arrived, Ethan pressed fifteen. When it dinged, he led Evie to his door.

She had barely entered before a barreling mound of fur was lunging at her.

"Oh god, Henry. Off! Off, Henry! I'm so sorry, Evie…"

But Evie was sitting on the floor rubbing Henry's face in her hands. He was immediately calm.

"I forgot you had a puppy." She was scratching Henry all over.

Henry laid down next to her, begging for belly rubs.

"I can't believe he calmed down," Ethan said, surprised.

"You just gotta get on their level." She bent towards Henry and he licked her nose. He didn't seem to remember his guardian.

Ethan sat on the floor too. "Guess I'm chopped liver then."

Henry perked up and trotted over to lick Ethan's face.

After a minute of snuggling the dog, he said, "Okay, buddy, bed."

"Doesn't he need to walk?" Evie said as Henry trotted to his bed.

"Nah, the dog walker came. He'll go out again in the morning."

"He's totally precious."

"Thanks. I think so."

He turned on a few lamps while Evie lingered at the doorway.

"So. This is the place," she said. She toyed with the strap of her bag, feeling slightly awkward.

"Yeah, come on in. Make yourself at home, I'll give you a tour." His hand was warm on the small of her back as he guided her through the apartment.

A brick wall ran the side of the open living area, from the kitchen to the floor-to-ceiling windows that opened onto a balcony. The kitchen's gleaming surfaces had the usual appliances on them, along with a bowl of fresh fruit. The living room was modern and masculine, with select, stylish pieces. A small upright piano stood in the corner, a guitar on a stand next to it.

Ethan put his arm around her waist, guiding her through the living area and towards his bedroom. It was inviting, with a brick wall on the opposite end, a king size bed with books and scripts piled on the nightstands next to it. A large chair and full-length mirror sat in the corner, and behind them the windows were covered with thin curtains. At the foot of the bed was a leather bench.

Evie ran her hand over the leather and cocked a brow. "Very manly."

He chuckled and puffed out his chest. "Just call me Gaston."

She snorted and opened the door to his bathroom, daring him to stop her with her with a look.

"I'm an open book. All you'll find is hair products," he said, seeming to accept her challenge.

She closed the door and moved to the next. She gasped when she opened it. "This is the most beautiful closet I have ever seen." She breathed reverently. The walk-in closet was stunning. His clothes were arranged by color, style, and type and she couldn't contain her glee. "You're a neat freak."

"I am and I'm proud."

"I knew I liked you."

Evie moved out of the closet, brushing Ethan's torso with her hand as she went by. She wandered back to the living room and stood before the ample bookshelf filled with novels. She was thrilled to discover that he was an avid reader.

"Do you like to read?" he said.

"Devoutly." She ran her hands over his well-worn copies of the *Song of Ice and Fire* series, including *A Game of Thrones.* His interests seemed vast--plenty of sci-fi and fantasy, political biographies, social justice essay collections. Many of his books, she'd read herself. Flipping through a worn script from a play he'd done between his first national tour and Broadway, she was charmed by the meticulous notes he'd made in fading pencil. His handwriting was small and neat. Character motivation was clearly important to him, and he seemed to be incredibly passionate about diving deep into his work.

Pleasantly surprised at how open he was, she caught his eye as she returned the script. He was smiling softly at her.

"There was talk of cheesecake?"

Ethan clapped his hands together. "There was, and far be it for me to make a liar of myself." He went to the fridge and she peeked into his guest room off the kitchen.

"This is an exceptional apartment."

"Thank you. I need a place I can call home that really feels like I live there."

"It feels like you. I mean, I know I barely know you. But it feels like you live here."

He paused with the Tupperware in his hand. "Thank you," he said, looking into her eyes.

When another one of those loaded silences came over them, she began to open drawers in the kitchen until she found the forks. Evie took one of the plates of cheesecake and went to sit on the floor in front of the island, facing the windows.

"Whatcha doin' down there?"

"Dessert after a night of whiskey is best eaten on the floor," she said matter-of-factly.

Ethan shrugged, clicked off the lamps, and sat facing her, his leg running the length of hers.

She hit him full force with a bright smile which he returned. She took a bite of cheesecake. "Are you kidding, Mrs. Carter? This is amazing."

He pushed his fork into his own slice. "I'll tell her you loved it."

"Seriously. This is excellent." Evie lost herself in the delicious dessert until Henry came over to investigate.

"Not for you, buddy, lay down," Ethan said.

Henry whined and laid down a foot away from their legs.

"He's really well behaved."

"Thank you, we've been working hard. He's pretty smart, so it's been easy," he said.

She simply smiled and set her empty plate on the floor.

He piled his on top and scooted a little closer to her. He twirled a piece of her hair between his fingers. "I *like* you." He sounded surprised.

"Right? I was so not expecting tonight to play out this way. I *like* you."

"Me neither. I have never--and I mean *ever*--invited a fan out for a drink. But there's..." He paused, as if remembering her past, remembering she didn't live in New York.

"What?"

His blue eyes shone at her in the moonlight coming through the windows. "I just want to remain sensitive. Of your past."

"I appreciate that. If you had told me six months ago that I would feel completely comfortable eating cheesecake on Ethan Carter's floor at midnight, I'd call you a liar."

His eyebrows went up. "You're completely comfortable?"

She looked toward the ceiling, while assessing what her body was feeling. "Weirdly and completely, yes," she said after a few moments.

"Same," he said quietly. He moved even closer to her. "There's something here. Or am I too wrapped up in wanting there to be?"

"You are not wrong. There's definitely something here," Evie concurred.

"Despite the complications."

"Despite those."

"You don't live here."

"My previous relationship did not end well."

"My career could take me literally anywhere for months at a time."

"Complicated," she whispered.

"Complicated," he responded in kind.

Her nose almost brushed his. "Do you know what I've learned though?" she said.

He traced her cheek with his thumb, then her lips, staring intently at them. "What?"

"Life is wildly unpredictable. And if you find a piece of happiness, you should hold on to it. For as long as you are allowed."

47

"Well then..." He leaned in to kiss her.

She stopped him with her forefinger on his lips. "Don't kiss me. Not yet."

He retreated, looking at her curiously, as if inviting her to explain.

"If you kiss me right now, there's no way we're not making use of that beautiful king bed in there," she murmured. "You see, I went through a period when I thought I would never get a first kiss again." As she said this, she moved slowly, changing her position.

He supported himself with his muscular arms as she moved over him.

Her lips were impossibly close to his, her warmth pressing into his chest, so close but not quite touching.

"It didn't make me sad at the time, but...I get to do that again, the anticipation...that thrill. I don't want to rush it. And if, as I think you might, you want to see me again while I'm here, let's...delay gratification.

"Can you imagine..." she breathed, "how incredible it will feel...later?"

"Tantric," he breathed. "You're a goddamn wonder."

She smiled slowly, letting her lips part. "They say that allowing delayed gratification is a sign of maturity." She ran her hand under his shirt, brushing it just along the top of his jeans, barely connecting with his skin, which felt almost on fire.

"Fuuuuuck." He exhaled as her hand pulled away.

"Later," she whispered, and nipped his earlobe.

He gasped. In one movement he had her under him, his hand just high enough on her thigh. He was holding himself above her with one arm. She trembled a little when he leaned down and breathed on her neck, over her collarbone, and took just one tiny bite of the freckles on her shoulder.

It was her turn to gasp. "Oh, this is gonna be good."

He grinned and moved his hand up her thigh.

Henry let out a yip.

They both laughed, and the intensity eased. As if connected, they sat up, their eyes smoldering.

"Well. I should get a cab," Evie said after a few charged moments, not wanting the night to end, but not wanting to overstay her welcome. Or get herself into something that could change her world again.

"What? No way," Ethan said. "Stay. Please?"

"You do have a spare room..."

Ethan shook his head. "No. Just..." He sounded both in pain and surprised. "Stay with me tonight. Breathe next to me." His eyes pled with her.

She touched his face, wondering at the angle of his jaw, the smile lines just deep enough to see. "Are you sure?"

He brushed his nose against hers. "Yes."

She put her forehead against his and inhaled deeply, making her decision. "I'd like that."

He let out a breath. Then his smile lit up like the moon outside.

CHAPTER SIX ♫

Evie returned Ethan's bright smile. "I'll have to text Daniel and let him know you are almost definitely not a serial killer." She walked over to her bag where she'd dropped it when she met the over-enthusiastic puppy. As she scrolled through the increasingly desperate texts, she laughed. "Oh man. Danny definitely thinks I'm dead. Poor guy."

She typed quickly.

> Baby, I'm fine, Ethan is a dream. Not coming back tonight. Call me after your auditions tomorrow. Break legs! Xxx

An immediate response followed.

> EVELYN I SWEAR TO GOD. DON'T DO THAT TO ME EVER AGAIN. Get yours babe, love you. Full report tomorrow. PS: get dirt on Max. I think we like each other. He's hot.

She looked over at Ethan, who was watching her intently. "A request for dirt on Max. What's his story?"

"Single and ready," Ethan replied.

"Excellent." After Evie sent another text, she and Ethan stood gazing at each other, the weirdness of what they were doing sinking in. "So... I don't have any clothes? Or a toothbrush? What's a gal to do?"

"Ah, well, lucky for you, I am a wonderful host," Ethan said in an English accent. He took on the air of the lord of a great manor. "You will find brand new toothbrushes and a number of other amenities in the guest bathroom, clean towels in the cabinet, and of course, please help yourself to any water, coffee, or juice, at any time."

Evie snickered and responded in an accent of her own. "That will be agreeable, your grace."

He went into the bedroom and came out with a gray v-neck t-shirt. "And, you'll be pleased to note, this is the softest t-shirt I own. I am allowing you to borrow it, which is very gracious of me, and for which I should be rewarded handsomely." He presented the shirt to her with a haughty flourish. "Will you be requiring boxers, m'lady?"

"I shan't. This will do nicely, your highness," she curtseyed, flashed him a bit of her underwear--black boy shorts, sensible--and retreated to the guest bath.

Ethan groaned. "I'm not feeling very mature," he yelled through the door.

"I have a feeling it'll be worth it," Evie called, and grinned to herself.

Looking in the mirror, she paused. Raising a hand up, she palmed the wedding bands on the chain around her neck. After a deep breath, she removed the necklace and folded her fingers around it. She kissed her fist and placed the rings gently in a zippered pocket of her bag. After washing her face and brushing her teeth, she momentarily wondered what the hell she was doing. This thing with Ethan was new but comfortable. Weird but not weird.

She put on his t-shirt. It was incredibly soft.

He retreated to his own bathroom, washed his face, flossed and brushed his teeth, and stripped down to his boxers. After turning the bedside lamp on, he set both of their phones to charge, proving that he was indeed a gracious host. As he did, he thought about that whole bit they'd just done, the nerdy Lord and Lady thing, and how Evie had played right along. He couldn't help comparing Evie to Paige, whose disdain of his goofy side was obvious. He and Evie seemed far more compatible in that department.

Evie appeared in the doorway with Henry, her hair plaited down her back in a long braid, braless in his thin shirt. He let out a heavy breath. She walked over to the bed, deliberately straddling over him to get to the other side, smiling deviously.

"You are..." he said, as she paused above him and he ran a hand up her thigh. "You know exactly what you're doing."

"I do. And so do you." She moved to her side of the bed.

He chuckled and turned off the lamp. Henry jumped up and sprawled at the end of the bed. The clock glowed 1:35 a.m.

As it had outside the bar, the environment shifted, something quiet replacing the heated intensity between them.

"You know we've only known each other for like, four hours?" he said as he spooned himself around Evie's body. He snaked his arm over her and caught her hand. A perfect fit.

"This is bizarre," she said softly.

"Weird but not weird," he agreed.

"Quite a view," Evie said quietly, as the city twinkled at them through the gauzy curtains. A sweet silence fell.

"You're like him, you know...Liam," Evie said a few moments later.

Ethan considered this.

After a while she said, "Steady. Kind. Genuine. Total nerdy weirdo."

Ethan smiled slightly, realizing her words weren't a comparison, but a compliment. He kissed her shoulder. "Thank you," he whispered.

She squeezed his hand, and he held her until her breathing grew slow and steady, and every one of her fingers relaxed in his.

§

Evie gasped and sat up in bed. She hadn't slept well since Liam's death, and tonight was no exception. She placed her hand over her heart and used the breathing techniques she'd learned from Dr. Reichs. After a few moments, she remembered where she was. She looked to her left, to the first person she'd slept next to in a year.

Ethan was sleeping deeply. His chest was bare, an arm flung above his head. His breathing was steady and even, his face peaceful. Evie matched her own breath to his and her pulse slowed. She laid back down, facing his Roman profile, and laid a hand on his chest. He shifted, his hand finding hers, but slept on.

She breathed along with him. After a while she felt herself drifting to sleep instead of lying awake and fighting her body, insisting it shut down. Her breathing evened out. Something had definitely changed.

§

Ethan felt the sun coming through the curtains and rolled over, opening his eyes. The bedside clock informed him it was 9:00 a.m. Henry trotted into the bedroom looking for all the world like he was saying, "It's time for a walk, Dad." Ethan smiled and ruffled his head, then looked over to his right.

Evie was on her side, facing away from him. He could tell she was sleeping deeply, and his heart swelled. Not wanting to wake her, he quickly put on joggers and a tee shirt, brushed his teeth, and wrote a note.

Took Henry out. Be right back. - E

He left it on the nightstand next to her.

As quietly as he could, he set coffee to brew and another little thrill ran through him as he made enough for two. As soon as they were outdoors, Henry trotted happily along and looked back at his guardian with a doggy smile.

"I know, buddy. She's pretty special," Ethan said to the happy pup.

When they returned, Evie still hadn't moved. Ethan chuckled while he gave Henry his breakfast. He poured the coffee into a decanter. He brought that and two mugs to his bedside table. After retrieving his laptop from the living room, he climbed back into bed, wearing his black framed glasses. A dozen emails greeted him from his publicist, his agent, a few friends.

After gobbling his food, Henry hopped up and snuggled against Evie's sleeping form. She stirred and rolled over, putting an arm over the dog. Eyes still closed, she smiled and rubbed his neck. He flopped onto his back, offering his belly. She chuckled and rubbed it, before opening her eyes.

"Henry, you're kind of slutty," she said. When he licked her nose in response, she giggled. She looked up at Ethan. "Hey, glasses," she said sleepily.

"Hey, Freckles."

"What time is it?"

"About nine-thirty."

"Wow. That was an incredible night's sleep. This bed is perfection," she said, and stretched.

"Told you I was a good host."

She sat up. "Whatcha doin'?"

"Taking care of business, like a boss." He reached over and poured her a cup of coffee as she scooted closer to peek at his screen. She accepted the mug and closed her eyes, clearly relishing the scent. She took a sip.

"You're perfect," she sighed. He put his arm around her and looked at the screen. She cuddled up next to him and followed his glance.

"Ooh, a review of the show! Did you know they would review it?"

"Not really, and it's pretty editorialized; it's just a Broadway blog. But I *am* impeccably charming and handsome and funny and talented."

"Don't forget humble," she teased.

"Exceedingly humble. And you got a shout out."

"What?" She straightened up.

"Yep. 'Carter sang a fan favorite, a song about having a crush on an Irish girl. As he sang, he charmed some audience members, including a pretty red-haired girl with whom he bantered back and forth when the song ended.'"

"Ooh, 'bantered'. Scandalous." Evie raised her eyebrows at him.

He chuckled and read on. "'As the show continued, maybe it was just this blogger's imagination, but Carter seemed to be catching the eye of the redhead a lot. Perhaps love is in the air, but I didn't stick around to find out. No one wants that hunk off the market!' Ah, good. The blogs will be wondering who you are now." He rolled his eyes and sighed.

"So what? Speculation is just speculation," Evie said sensibly. "No one knows that wasn't the end of it."

"I just...don't like that. My private life is private."

"Okay," she countered, "but aren't rumors just rumors? I mean, no one saw us leave, and if anyone saw us at the bar, still only your doorman and the cab driver know I came home with you."

"True. And the doorman has an NDA," Ethan reasoned.

"Really? Smart."

"I just try to control as much of what the public knows about me as possible. Only you discerned that my relationship ended...it seems that way anyway. And there are always rumors and speculation. But until something serious happens, I'm just not willing to--" He paused when Evie put a hand on his.

"I totally understand. I've had enough press to last a lifetime," she said, her voice thick.

Ethan hadn't considered that. Of course a young couple being torn apart in a tragic accident on a romantic vacation was press-worthy. He let the moment go. "You're pretty great," he said, and laid his hand on her cheek.

Her phone signaled an incoming text as she took his hand and kissed the inside of his wrist. "You're not so bad yourself."

She rolled over and grabbed her phone from the nightstand as he returned to his email. She began snickering as soon as she looked at the message. "Daniel would like a full penis report."

Ethan frowned at his screen. "Mmm." He kept typing, seemingly uninterested. "Flaccid or hard?"

Smiling slyly, she spoke aloud as she typed into her phone.

Oh, we're being full on tantric. No sexual activity yet, but I did get a great night's sleep. And I think we'll be seeing more of each other before we leave. Report forthcoming.

She paused and grinned at him, clearly excited about what the day would bring.

Break legs, call me later!

Evie stretched, and sat up. She got out of bed and headed for the guest bathroom, while making a show of pretending to dial a phone number.

Ethan glanced up, his eyebrows raised. "Calls to make?" He guessed what was coming.

"Mmm. Yes," she said when she was almost out the bedroom door. "Hello, yes, is this TMZ?"

He laughed and whipped a pillow at her.

She shrieked and ran.

After sending a final email, he took his last sip of coffee and headed to his bathroom.

A little later, Evie reappeared in Ethan's closet door, smiling. The scent of lavender wafted towards him. Her hair was piled on top of her head in a messy bun. She wore a black bralette and a towel around her waist.

He himself was only wearing jeans, with the fly still undone.

They stared at each other. He watched a flush creep up Evie's chest, felt his own breathing getting heavier, the longer they regarded each other's half naked bodies. He cleared his throat.

"So, what's your day look like?" he asked casually, while buttoning his jeans.

She grinned, clearly knowing she'd won whatever contest they were having.

"Free and clear. I was going to spend the day at the library. I've never been."

"Seriously?" he paused in putting on an undershirt.

"Yeah. But first I have to stop and get some clothes, seeing as how I only have last night's dress. Though I've never shied from the Walk of Triumph." She smirked and leaned against the door frame.

"I'd love to take you to the library. It's one of my favorite places."

"Really?" She sounded incredulous that he had nothing better to do.

He moved closer to her and wrapped her in a hug. "Absolutely."

Evie breathed deeply. "Mmm. Freshly showered man."

"In fact, if you just want to wear yesterday's dress for the next couple of hours, we could go have breakfast. I have a meeting with my publicist, but after that we could go to your place, and then to the library. And then have dinner tonight? And I'm just now realizing how ridiculous and relatively desperate I sound?" Feeling a bit vulnerable, he sat on the bench to slip on his shoes.

Evie walked into the closet and shut the door.

Feeling confused, Ethan stared at the closet door. "I know it's weird," he called, "but I'm… I mean, you're only here until Tuesday and I don't have much to do for the next couple of days, which is rare. And it's just that I really like you and I love the library, and I'm… I'm…totally feeling this, okay? And also, I really want to kiss you." He ran his hands through his hair, feeling like a teenager.

When Evie opened the closet door, she was wearing a pair of his tapered green joggers, rolled at the top to fit her hips and the bottom so she wouldn't trip all over them. She'd also put on a white button down, tied at her waist, the sleeves rolled up.

Ethan gaped.

"I hate wearing yesterday's clothes." She came to him and wrapped her arms around his waist. "I'm totally feeling this too," she said against his chest.

He smiled and closed his eyes. "Weird but not weird."

She nodded.

"How is it possible that you look that good in my clothes?"

"Buddy, I look good in everything."

"That right there. That confidence. My god, if you could bottle that…how did you get there?" he demanded.

"Ha! A lot of soul searching, not being in my twenties anymore, realizing nobody cares about me as much as I think they do. And the old *fake it til you make it* trope actually works."

"I hear that." He knew exactly what she meant.

"I'm starving."

"Same. Let's go."

He led her to the elevator and as soon as the doors closed, Ethan pushed her against the wall. One of his hands gripped her waist, the other pulled hers above her head. Bending over, he trailed his tongue lightly up her neck.

"Don't ever walk into my closet wearing only a towel again, you delicious little tease," he whispered into her ear.

She hooked her fingers into his belt loop and tugged his hips closer. "Don't ever order me around."

They locked eyes, challengers. Equals.

"There's something to be said for anticipation, but those doors better open soon or we're not waiting another second," he said, and pushed his hips against hers.

Evie smiled slowly while trailing her thumb against the top of his jeans, right above his hip bone.

He stepped away and bounced up and down for a moment, mumbling "The Yankees, the Red Sox, the Dodgers..."

She burst into laughter.

"Hey, I can't walk around aroused." He shot her a look filled with desire.

"That's true, but you started it. I'd be concerned about my underwear...but I'm not wearing any," she teased as the doors dinged open.

Ethan groaned under his breath and followed her out into the street.

"Whatever else happens, if I don't get you into bed before you leave Tuesday, I will consider that a great tragedy of my life," he growled in her ear.

"Oh, I don't think you have anything to worry about there," Evie said, grinning up at him.

"This is like a...What?" He checked his watch. "Twenty-four-hour seduction?" He didn't feel a need to mention that they'd definitely be together that evening.

Evie took his hand. "I guess so. I'm enjoying it, myself."

"Me too," he said with enthusiasm.

They took a cab to a diner in Manhattan, where they had omelets and more coffee. As they ate, they chatted about their lives, high school, theatre, and what Evie was thinking of doing with the rest of her life. They laughed together as they came up with more and more ridiculous jobs for her. At his insistence, Ethan paid the bill.

As they waited for the server to return with his card, Evie regarded him with a strange expression.

"What?" He rubbed his stubble. "Food on my face?"

"No. Familiarity. Like we do this every Saturday morning," Evie said.

Her bluntness took him by surprise. Ethan took her hand. "Isn't that... I mean...don't people..." He looked away, then back. The question he wanted to ask seemed too deep for brunch. He dropped her hand and picked at a napkin. Evie looked on, a curious look on her face.

"What?" she said.

Tossing the napkin aside, he ran a hand through his hair. He stacked their dishes, and then began to tap a spoon on the table. All the while, Evie watched, a bemused smile spreading across her face. He met her eyes and lost the battle he was having with himself.

"I don't know. I... I've honestly never felt so comfortable so quickly with someone before. I feel like I can really be myself with you, like I can tell you anything. This is new for me." He tossed down the spoon and sat back. "And see, I just keep telling you intimate things like I've known you forever and I haven't been telling my publicist how important my privacy is every ten minutes for the last five years." Realizing he'd been gesticulating broadly, he picked up a sugar packet and forced himself to be still.

Evie cocked an eyebrow at him.

"I just feel so normal with you, and I'm just wondering why...why do you think--" He faltered, trying to find the right words.

"Yeah," Evie said through a sigh, "Look. I knew I was going to marry Liam the second I saw his face." She glanced out the window and rubbed her brow, as if she couldn't believe the conversation they were having.

Ethan stared at her, not quite believing she had intuited what he wanted to know--how immediately love could happen. He felt terrified of this woman he'd known for less than a day. How had they gotten here? She still was not meeting his gaze and he kicked himself mentally. Tentatively, he reached for her hand.

"Evie, I didn't--"

"I know." Abruptly, she pulled her hand away, stood, and walked towards the bathroom. He stared after her, angry with himself. She was only here for the weekend, why did he complicate things?

§

In the ladies' room, Evie tried to clutch her necklace, where she'd gone for comfort when she needed it, and realized she had forgotten to put it on. It was in the bag that was still in the booth. She put a hand over her heart, feeling it beat a little too rapidly. Was panic going to set in? She took three deep breaths and reminded herself: she knew where the necklace was and could put it on when she got back to the table.

Glancing up into the mirror, she gripped the edge of the sink. "You deserve to move on. You deserve to be happy."

Three more deep breaths.

"Also, what the fuck, Evelyn, you've known him for about fifteen seconds. Get a grip."

§

While Evie was gone, Ethan left the tip and signed the sales slip, all the while wondering how he had gotten into this situation. He considered telling her that he didn't want to hurt her, or push her into anything, and that *of course* he didn't want to marry her. There was just something deeper here than what he'd anticipated there would be when he invited her backstage. He certainly hadn't thought he'd ask her to go for a drink. And he definitely hadn't thought he'd be taking her home or asking her to spend the night. He reminded himself not to get too attached. This was just a fling.

61

And then she walked back to the table and smiled at him.

That was all he needed to feel calm again.

"All set?" Evie reached for her bag and slung it over her shoulder. Relief passed over her face when she put her hand inside. She seemed to find what she was looking for.

"Let's go." He stood, reached for her hand without thinking, and they walked out into the Manhattan sunshine.

"So hey," Evie said, after a block of pleasant silence, "just as an FYI, you wouldn't be the first guy I've had sex with...since. So, no pressure or anything. It's not like I'm not going to get clingy or weird or cry a lot. I figured you'd want to know."

Ethan let out a breath. "Yeah, I kind of did. Thanks."

"Sorry if that's awkward."

"It's not. I mean--" He took a deep breath, stopped, and looked deep into her eyes, "I've also had sex."

"Whaaaat? I knew you were slutty."

"Hey, no, that's my dog." He joined her melodic laughter as he put his arm around her shoulders.

"Also, real quick, I have an IUD and I'm STI free. Just to get that out of the way, too."

"Me too...not the IUD, but no STI's." He let a devilish grin sneak across his face and put on his lord of the manor voice again. "I am very much looking forward to the mutual pleasure we will be partaking in tonight."

"Mm, yes, as am I," she purred up at him.

Suddenly, Ethan pulled her into a recessed doorway. "But there's no way I'm waiting another second to do this." He put his palms on the side of her face, pressed her against the wall, and molded his lips to hers.

She responded immediately, sliding her arms around his waist, pulling him to her. The world around him stopped, as their mouths opened, breaths mingled. They pulled apart after several seconds, both breathing heavily.

"Oh, holy shit," she said, her green eyes swimming with desire.

"Likewise," he said. "Guess you were right about not kissing last night. That was...wow..."

"Wow is right. Hey, you're not wearing a hat or sunglasses. Better keep an eye out, or you'll break Twitter if someone snaps a photo."

He chuckled. "Excellent point. What's next?"

"I still have to change my clothes," she said as they stepped out of the doorway together.

Ethan stuck out his lower lip. "But you look so cute in mine," he said and wrapped his arms around her.

She laughed up at him and kissed his pout. "Okay, my clothes can wait. Maybe I'll go meet Daniel."

"And I have to go meet my publicist in--" He checked his watch. "--twenty minutes. She doesn't come in on Saturday's often, so I can't be late."

He met her eyes and they both breathed in deeply.

What comes next? he wondered.

CHAPTER SEVEN ♫

"Okay," Evie said after several beats, "go to your meeting, and I'll meet you at the library afterwards." She squeezed his hand, still reeling a little from the kiss.

"Okay. And you'll meet up with Daniel?"

"Yeah," she said.

Ethan started to say something and hesitated.

"What?"

"I don't know, I feel like... This is so stupid... But if we part right now--"

"The spell will be broken and this will all go away?" she concluded.

"That exactly. And I can't believe how dumb that sounds." He rolled his eyes.

Evie put her hands on the sides of his face. "Trust me, Carter. If I don't get you in bed by Tuesday, I will consider it one of the greatest tragedies of my life." She rose to her tiptoes to kiss him lingeringly.

"Go do your thing. I'll see you at the library at two," Ethan said, and cupped her face in his hand.

"Think we should exchange numbers?"

"Ah, we haven't done that, have we?" Evie shook her head. He pulled out his phone, and she gave him her number. He started a text to her.

She saw his hesitation before he pressed SEND. "Hey, I totally understand if you don't want to do this. But I'm not going to give your number out, I promise. And I'm not going to call TMZ. That was a joke."

He looked into her eyes, and pressed SEND.

Her phone beeped. She crowed, "Victory. And now to make my millions."

She looked at his expression, which was stricken. "Oh god, Ethan, I'm sorry. Seriously... I would never. I promise."

He shook his head. "It's okay, really. Sorry. You know, it's the privacy thing."

"Never again," she promised sincerely.

He wrapped his arms around her in a tight hug. "Don't worry about it. I'd better get to my meeting."

Evie kissed him again. "Go get 'em, tiger."

He squeezed her hand before hailing a cab. As he climbed in, he glanced back at her. She sent him a text.

> Can't wait to sniff old books with you. And then get all kinds of naked.

He sent back:

> This meeting is going to go very slowly. See you on the steps of the palace.

She grinned at his *Into the Woods* reference and replied immediately.

> No need to spread any pitch. You've got me.

> Ditto.

65

Evie called Daniel.

"Tell me literally everything," he said, not even bothering with hello.

"I will, where are you? He's at a meeting, I'm at 71st and 5th, by the park."

"I'm near there. Meet me at Strawberry Fields?"

"See you in fifteen," she sang.

Evie made her way across Central Park, daydreaming about Ethan and enjoying the sunshine. She spotted Daniel twenty minutes later near the John Lennon memorial. "Hi baby."

"Okay, I swear to goddess, tell me everything. Now."

Evie hugged him tightly and together they sat on a bench. "First tell me how your audition went."

"Great, I think. I felt okay about it. I feel more prepared for this afternoon, for *Fully Engaged*. Callbacks are Monday for that one. If I get one, that really means something and it doesn't matter, you spent the night with *Ethan Carter*."

Evie gave him a brief summary of her evening, including the weirdness in the diner and the kiss.

"Sooo…what? He wants to marry you?" Daniel said when she was finished.

"No. That's not it. I think that he's feeling more than he usually feels. So am I, for sure. And I think it kind of scares us both. But it's just a fling. Only… A little more than a fling? It's literally been like fifteen hours, Danny."

Daniel took a deep breath and sat back on the bench. "That's intense."

"I know. Weird but not weird. We both said that."

"Hmm."

"Exactly." She toyed with the strap of her bag, gazing at the inlaid mosaic of the John Lennon memorial in front of her. *Imagine.*

"So, what's next?"

"We're going to the library together, and then to dinner, and we are definitely gonna get naked tonight." Evie felt her grin widen at that thought. "And we leave on Tuesday, so it'll be a great story for the rest of my life?"

Daniel laughed and put an arm around her.

She snuggled into him.

"What are you really feeling?" he said.

She sighed and considered, her thoughts swirling.

After a few moments' thought, she said, "I feel major attraction to him, but also really like him as a person. He's… He's like Liam, Daniel. He's good and goofy and generous and such a nerd. He's sweet and he's smart, and he seems to get me." She trailed off, her eyes filling with tears. "And maybe I'm just projecting, I don't know."

Daniel squeezed her closer. "I know, babe."

"Three hundred and eighty-three days."

"And every one of them better than the last," Daniel said softly.

Evie stiffened, her shoulders tensing up. "I'm betraying him." she said, feeling the warmth leave her body.

"You are not. Were you when you slept with what's-his-name?" Daniel said.

She shook her head. "Gross. No. That was… I just needed to get that out of my system."

"And those dates you went on? Did you feel like you were betraying him then?"

"Kind of." She paused to think about the couple of men she'd gone out with. "I guess not. But I also knew those guys weren't going to be meaningful relationships."

"Well, neither is Ethan, is he?" Daniel asked gently.

Evie wiped her eyes, after a moment's consideration. "I suppose not. No. I mean, it can't."

"Look at me," Daniel said.

When Evie turned to him, he took her face in his hands and wiped her tears. "Liam was a wonderful man. But Liam is gone. And we both miss him. Evelyn, you deserve to move on. You deserve to be happy, whether it's with some other guy or Ethan-fucking-Carter. Whatever happens this week, it's just another step in your healing process. I know you still grieve for Liam, but you can find happiness, too. The two aren't mutually exclusive."

Evie gave him a small smile. "What would I do without you?"

Daniel kissed her forehead. "Keel over and die, I expect. Now, about Max--"

After talking with Daniel some more, Evie made her way to the library. She sat amid the tourists on the steps of the library, deep in thought. Her mind was spinning with everything that had happened in the last day. Her heart, although still grieving, raced at the thought of Ethan's smile and his hand in hers. She wasn't sure what she was doing, but she knew she wanted to continue. It wasn't what she had planned. She'd thought she would go to the show and make eyes at Ethan for a bit, and then go get a drink with Daniel. She'd thought she'd tool around New York for the next few days, and then go home.

She wrapped a stray strand of hair around her finger and bit her lip. She decided to take Dr. Reich's advice. It was time to start letting life happen.

§

Ethan entered a sleek building on Fifth Avenue.

The receptionist smiled when he walked in and made a call. "Julie will be out in a second, Ethan," she said as she replaced the receiver.

"Thanks, Allie." He sat and scrolled through the few texts he and Evie had exchanged, smiling to himself.

"Hey, Ethan," Julie said as she entered the lobby. "How are you, my friend?"

Ethan hugged her. "Hey Jules, I'm great."

Once in her office, they discussed strategy for his upcoming live shows, a few interviews she had set up in the cities he was going to and went over a few photos for promotional materials. She asked about auditions.

"I've got a few coming up. One is for a Netflix show, so that would be awesome. And I'm in the running to play

Wesley in a workshop of *The Princess Bride* musical. Hopefully, something pans out. I miss working steadily."

"I know. At least you have this tour to occupy you until it happens. And I heard you had a great show last night," Julie said as they were wrapping up.

"Yeah. It was a fantastic crowd," Ethan said. He looked away from her and clasped his hands together. She couldn't have known anything beyond what the blog review said.

Julie smirked and crossed her arms. "So-- Who's the redhead?"

Ethan sat back, still not meeting her eyes. He shrugged. "Oh, just a fan. Fun to play with. I invited her backstage to say hello. She's lovely."

Julie just raised an eyebrow. "And?"

Ethan hesitated. "And..." he drawled.

"Ethan, it's my job to know this kind of thing," Julie said seriously, but with warmth. Ethan stood and went to the window. He knew he could trust Julie, as he had for five years. He took a deep breath.

"Okay, so...*and* I invited her for a drink...*and* we went for a walk...*and* we went back to my apartment...*and* she spent the night...*and* we just had breakfast...*and* I'm meeting her later. That's it." Turning from the window, his palms up, he gave her his famous smile.

Julie's eyes widened but she was grinning.

"Ethan! That's a big deal. Your doorman is still under his NDA, correct?"

"Of course."

"Okay. And there's nothing on social media this morning but the review and sneaky videos of the show. So, you're still protected. But be cautious, okay? We don't want any other...problems."

Ethan nodded slowly. "Yeah. Yeah, I mean, it's New York. No one really notices me here. Not that often, anyway." He caught her eye and a moment of shared tension passed between them.

"Just keep me posted if something happens and I'll do my best to keep it under wraps."

"Will do." Ethan gave her a slightly shaky smile.

Julie tapped some papers on her desk and grinned. "So. She's special, huh?"

Leaning back, Ethan ran his hands through his hair. "You know that thing girls do in movies? They meet a cute guy and then they run around their apartment, all giddy and squealing?"

"Absolutely."

"That's what I'm feeling. Totally giddy. I *like* her. I haven't liked a woman in a long time. Not like this," he said. "But anyway, she lives in Chicago, so it's just a fling. Nothing serious. I mean, it can't be, there's a lot of other stuff too, so it's not like I'm going to be dating her. Just…until Tuesday, I'm having a great time."

Julie seemed pleased, but ever the professional, brought up a complication. "One last thing before I let you out of here. Do you still plan on going to the Broadway Cares gala on Monday night? It's their biggest benefit of the year, so I'm assuming you don't want to miss it."

Ethan smiled at the mention of his favorite charity. "I almost forgot about that. I'm in. Maybe I'll bring Evie."

Julie's eyebrows shot up. He hadn't expressed an interest in bringing a date to anything in two years.

"Okay, if that's the case, two things. Obviously, there will be photographs and press, including a step-and-repeat. She will be visible, and then likely Googled until the end of time, if anyone finds out her name. Your fans will take any scrap of information and run with it. She should know what she's walking into, and that the scrutiny can be intense."

He hadn't even meant to invite Evie. It had seemed like the natural thing to do and just popped out of his mouth. "I'll consider every angle, I promise. I wouldn't put her in a difficult situation on purpose."

"I know you wouldn't, but again, it's my job."

He grinned at her. "And you're good at it, and I appreciate you."

"Second thing. I just heard from Paige's rep, and she'll be there."

Ethan let out a breath. His industry friends knew that he and Paige had dated, and they knew about the drama of the breakup, thanks to Paige's eagerness to share it with the world. Paige's girlfriends certainly thought he was a huge asshole.

He shrugged, gritting his teeth. "So, if I don't go, it'll look like I didn't because of her and that I don't care about fighting AIDS. If I do go, I'll have to see her, with the potential for drama. And if I do go with Evie, it'll be that times ten."

Julie nodded. "Basically."

Ethan tapped his fingers on the arms of his chair. "I will go; I'm not letting Paige scare me away from things I want to do. But I'll think about asking Evie."

"I'll put you in with a plus one, just in case you decide to invite her," Julie said, and typed into her computer.

Ethan rolled his eyes and rubbed his palms over his face. "Why'd you ever let me get involved with Paige?"

She gave him an indulgent grin. "Ethan, if I've learned anything in five years, it's that you do whatever the hell you want. I just try to guide you in the right direction."

"Thanks, Jules. Text me the details. I'll talk to you later?"

"I'll be in touch."

As he exited her office, he heard her chuckle.

Ethan had felt a rush from telling Julie about Evie. Once in a cab on his way to the library, he smiled like a goon.

He paused when he saw Evie sitting on the steps, wearing his clothes. She had a slight frown on her face. He watched as she twirled her hair in her fingers and felt a warmth spread in his chest.

"No gold shoes, Cinderella?" he asked her as he approached, his shadow falling across her. She smiled up at him.

"I appreciate Sondheim sticking to the Grimm fairy tale. Gold shoes make so much more sense than glass slippers. And I told you. You've already got me."

"Your musical theatre reference game is on point."

"I pride myself on that. Thank you." She grinned at the compliment.

He offered his hand, and she took it. They walked up the steps and into the cool, still air of the library.

"Ohhh..." Evie breathed as she looked around the grand room, the desks lining the middle and the shelves and shelves of books lining the walls.

"Come on," he said, and tugged her hand, excited about his surprise. They approached the front desk. "Hi, I'm here to see Fareed," he said to the woman behind it.

"Oh, of course, you must be Mr. Carter. I'll call him up."

When Evie looked at Ethan, a dozen questions on her face, he smiled secretively. "Turns out my publicist has some pull here."

Before leaving the building, he had doubled back to Julie's office to ask her if there was a way to get a private tour of the library. Happily, she did know someone in the Stephen A. Schwarzman press office, and while he was in the cab on his way over, she had made a call. He'd received the confirmation text as he exited the cab.

Evie turned excitedly to him. "What?"

"Patience," he told her.

A young docent in a blue jacket approached, his hand held out.

"Mr. Carter, it's such a pleasure. I'm happy to take you on your private tour. My name is Fareed."

"Thank you for doing this on such short notice, Fareed. And please, Ethan is fine. This is Evie."

"Oh my gosh, this is incredible. Ethan, thank you."

"Shall we get started?" Fareed said.

Evie bounced on the balls of her feet and, as if forgetting about discretion, she kissed Ethan on the cheek. "You're something else, Carter."

Fareed led them off on their tour.

For the next two hours, they marveled at the grand rooms, the Rose Main Reading Room, the exhibits, the event spaces, and the best part, the smell of old books.

Ethan thanked Fareed when he left them in the stacks to wander a bit more. Evie's hand was warm in his and he enjoyed seeing the library through her eyes. She appeared to be as enamored with it as he was. After a bit more time meandering together, he followed her outside.

It was just after five o'clock, and Saturday commuters were on the move among the tourists. They stood at the top of the steps adjusting to the fast pace after an afternoon of quiet and peace.

"That was one of the nicest things anyone has ever done for me. Thank you," Evie said.

"You're a wonderful person."

"So are you. Sincerely, that was such a treat."

Ethan felt himself blush a little. He was used to compliments from a lot of different people, and most of the time, he felt there was some ulterior motive for them. Evie spoke with such candor, proving what she had told him in the green room the night before. Life is too short to mince words.

She nestled into him, tucking herself under his chin. He put his arm around her waist, not wanting the magic of the moment to pass.

"Hey," she said. She pulled back and he met her eyes.

"Hey," he replied.

A loaded moment passed between them before Evie broke the silence.

"So… I'm getting hungry and I need to get back to our AirBnB and change for dinner."

"Yeah, I'm famished. And I know this great little place to take you over by my building. Really good Italian food. Is that okay?"

"*In omnia paratus.*"

He pulled back, once again amazed by her. "What? Did you just speak Latin?"

"Don't be that impressed, it's from *Gilmore Girls*."

"What does it mean?"

She pressed the length of her body against him, reached up on her tiptoes, and put her hands on either side of his face. Looking into his eyes, she said, "Ready for anything."

He kissed her deeply.

CHAPTER EIGHT ♫

The evening sky was beginning to turn pink with the setting sun as they wandered up Fifth Avenue. Evie slid her arm around Ethan's waist, and he put his arm around her shoulders. Evie's spirits were high after a lovely afternoon spent so quietly together. Ethan's calm silence led her to believe he felt the same.

"We're good at companionable silence," she said after they walked a couple of blocks.

"We are. What do you suppose that's about?"

"You can laugh at me, but I firmly believe there's a reason why people come into our lives... and maybe right now, you and I are supposed to be together."

"I'm on board with that," he said.

"Really?"

"Actually--" He took a breath. "--that is one of my main tenets. I don't think there's anyone I've met who hasn't been in my life at the exact right moment. Even the shitty ones."

"Well. Write that down as another thing we have in common, then," she said.

After a few more blocks, they took a cab to Evie's AirBnB. She texted Daniel to let him know they were coming by. He replied that he had just returned from his audition and looked forward to seeing them.

"Hello, young lovers," he sang as they walked in the door.

Evie laughed and kissed him on the cheek.

Ethan whistled at the impressive condo. "Damn. Living the high life on the Upper East Side. Hi, Daniel."

"Hey, Ethan. Nice to see you again."

"How was the last audition?" Evie said.

"It went really well. A little better than the one this morning. Now I wait. Am I to assume you're standing me up for the show tonight, Evie?"

She gestured at Ethan. "You know very well I'm not going. Look at him."

Daniel gave her a wink. "Makes sense to me. Maybe I'll see if Max wants to go tonight."

This elicited a big smile from Ethan. "I'm sure he'd be thrilled."

"I hope you get a callback from both productions. You definitely deserve it, you've worked so hard," Evie said. She hugged him. "I'm going to go change."

She went into her bedroom and heard Ethan and Daniel chat about Daniel's chances of getting the part in *Fully Engaged*. Opening her suitcase, she chose a black maxi dress. She pulled off Ethan's clothes and put it on. In the bathroom, she took her hair down, and with the help of a little dry shampoo, it fell down her back in waves. She reached into her bag and put her necklace on, tucking the rings into her dress. Finally, she put her Chucks on her feet and walked back to the living room.

Ethan and Daniel both whistled.

"You know that's my favorite thing about a maxi? You put on literally two pieces of clothing and it makes you look like you made tons of effort," she said as she posed for them.

"You look beautiful as always, babe. I'm going to shower for my big night with Max, stage manager extraordinaire. You kids have fun tonight."

"Bye, Daniel. Love you," Evie said.

"Love you, princess, have a good night." He wrapped her in a warm hug and whispered in her ear. "Be happy." He straightened up and pointed at Ethan. "Take care of my girl."

Ethan touched two fingers to his forehead in a quick salute.

Daniel grinned at him and retreated to his room.

Ethan turned his attention to Evie, his brows knitted together, frowning slightly.

Evie eyed him curiously. "The hell is that look?"

"Just... if we're leaning into this whole fling thing, why don't you just bring all your stuff with you? I mean, you're obviously staying tonight. Why not the rest of the weekend?" He stepped closer to her and raised her hand to his lips. He kissed the inside of her wrist, and then moved his other hand to her waist, pulling her to him.

She reached up and tangled her fingers in his thick hair. His blue eyes searched hers, as if for an answer. She rose up and kissed him slowly. All the thoughts that had been swirling since she met him suddenly seemed to stop. Everything she needed to know was in his kiss. With a passion that surprised her, she drew him closer, deepening their embrace.

His hands found the bare skin of her back and he ran his fingers lightly down her spine. She paused, gasping, and drew back. His blue eyes bored into hers and he fervently kissed her again. She slid her hands under his shirt, feeling the taut muscles of his back. He groaned.

Picking her up with apparent ease, he carried her to the couch.

Sitting down so she straddled his hips, Ethan put a hand on her neck and drew her to him, a burning look in his eyes. The dress bunched up around her waist as he moved his hands up her thighs. She felt pleasure to the tips of her toes and scooted towards him, unable to feel enough of him, wanting him closer. Everything else seemed to melt away, her worries for the future, her grip on the past. When Ethan was kissing her, all felt right in the world, something she never thought she would experience again.

She felt his erection through his jeans and couldn't help smiling. She pulled back a bit, breathless, and laughed, low and sexy.

"Excuse me, madam, what the fuck are you laughing at?" Ethan's chest rose and fell rapidly, his cheeks flushed.

She bit his bottom lip.

"Just that my report to Daniel is surely going to be satisfactory," she murmured.

He laughed low, practically a growl, and kissed her a bit more chastely. "We better go or we're never leaving. Unless you just wanna get the awkward first time out of the way now."

"I don't think there's going to be anything awkward, if the last few minutes is any indication."

"Fair point. Does this mean you're staying with me for the rest of your trip?"

"Absolutely." She disentangled her dress and stood.

Ethan raised his eyes to the ceiling and mumbled baseball stats.

"Wow, I really have an effect on you. Does baseball really work?"

"It will if you stop standing there being all perfect." He took her hand and kissed it.

Evie tingled all over. *This is pretty perfect.* She turned to go pack up her things.

§

Looking out at the skyline from Ethan's apartment windows, Evie picked at a bowl of grapes. He had taken Henry for a walk. Once he had gone, a sigh escaped her and she put a hand to her chest. Under her dress, she could feel the rings warm against her skin. She closed her eyes, allowing her breathing to deepen. After a few moments, she turned and took in Ethan's home. Next to his TV, Playbills hung in frames, all shows she had seen various productions of and loved.

She ran her hand over the back of an armchair, one that looked a lot like a chair in her own living room. Settling into it, she tucked her feet underneath herself and plucked another grape.

She rubbed the nape of her neck, where Ethan's hand fit perfectly. And where her necklace rested.

Drawing the chain out of her dress, she looked at the rings. It felt strange to wear them tonight. Her heartbeat quickened as she removed the necklace and put it into her bag.

A few minutes later, the sound of paws on the hardwood floor interrupted her reverie. Henry danced around the counter and Ethan gave him a treat.

A warmth spread through her, leaving her lips curved into a smile.

Slowly, he walked over to her and offered his hand. "What's on your mind?"

She stood and put her arms around him, tilting her face up to his. His soft lips met hers and once again, everything else fell away.

Ethan pulled back slowly. "I like that you smile when you kiss me. I'm going to change and then I can make us a cocktail before we go."

"That sounds good." As he walked to the bedroom, she put the grapes back in the fridge.

Evie whistled at him when he returned to the living room a few minutes later, a gray blazer over his t-shirt.

He imitated her pose from earlier.

She held up an imaginary camera. "Mr. Carter, who are you wearing?"

"The jacket is Calvin Klein, the t-shirt is a very fancy brand called Hanes." He began rummaging around a cupboard and mixed them each a drink.

Evie accepted hers and clinked his glass. "To us. And a fabulous weekend."

"To us." His gaze locked on hers and he looked quite pleased when she sighed with pleasure after a sip.

"Delicious. What is it?"

"Seven and seven, but my secret ingredient is a splash of bitters."

"Clever. I like it."

He guided her out onto the balcony, where they reclined on the wicker chairs. A shiver went through her when his hand found hers, his thumb tracing her palm. She met his eyes.

"Evie," Ethan said. "You're a wonder. I know it hasn't been twenty-four hours yet, but this is by far the best I've felt with a woman in a very long time."

A contentment spread through her. "Me too." She took another sip of her cocktail. "I'm so glad you hit on me during your show."

"I did not hit on you. I was simply playing to a good audience. Who happened to be gorgeous." He took a sip of his drink. "And funny."

"Please," she said, stretching the word out. "You wanted me immediately."

"You bet I did. What a surprise you've turned out to be." He pulled out his phone. "Would it be weird to take a photo? We only have a few days, and I want to remember them."

"Really? I thought you would be anti-photo."

"Nah, I love them. I just don't put them on the internet. But I know I'll regret not having one of the two of us."

"Okay, then, let's do it." They stood, with backs against the balcony. Ethan put his arm around her.

He snapped a couple of selfies and then scrolled through them. "You are wildly photogenic."

"Thanks. And have you *seen* you?"

"My lady, how forward," he mocked in his lord of the manor accent, his hand over his heart.

"I'll show you forward." Flinging her arms around his neck, she pressed her lips to his for a few delicious moments.

Ethan pulled slowly away from her. "I know I said I was famished earlier, but it's gone beyond hyperbole. You ready?"

"Definitely. Let's go."

After walking for a few blocks, Ethan ushered Evie through the door of the Italian restaurant. Modern light fixtures hung low from the ceiling, bathing the contemporary furniture and exposed brick in a romantic glow. The host led them to a table in a corner, where Ethan sat with his back to the room. He did not want to be recognized, not tonight.

Evie's eyes danced in the candlelight.

The server arrived with a breadbasket and Ethan asked Evie to choose the wine. When it arrived, he lifted his glass. "To us, again."

"To us, again." The glasses chimed.

The pinot noir was fruity and slightly dry and Ethan savored it. "Excellent choice."

"Thank you," Evie said. She sat back a bit, seeming to consider something. "So Carter, what are you looking for in a partner?"

Taken aback, he set his glass down and peered at her. This question was deeper than he expected. The look she gave him was a dare. He cleared his throat and picked at a piece of bread as he pondered for a moment.

"Well, a reader. And a critical thinker. Someone who likes to be active. She doesn't have to be into everything I that am, but she should be supportive."

"It's really important to have separate interests, in my opinion, and support them even if you're not into them. Especially when one of those interests is *bowling*." She snorted over her wine glass.

He threw a piece of bread at her.

"Definitely," he paused, still thinking. "Someone interested in social justice. Someone who gets my humor, and my goofy side. And someone who can tolerate my schedule, obviously."

She nodded. "Of course."

"It's been hard. I mean, I haven't met anyone in a long time who really clicked with me. I certainly had problems in my last relationship. She just didn't get me. But she tolerated my schedule. I think it was more that she liked the idea of being with Famous Ethan Carter rather than Ethan the guy."

"That's hard. Why did you stay with her?" Evie said.

"It was easy?" He shrugged. "I know that's not a great answer, but when we were together, she was... Well, most of the time she was fun. She got dramatic, and she was desperate for me to go public about her, but she got along with my friends. We didn't have a lot in common. I thought it was an 'opposites attract' situation. Turns out that was wrong."

"It happens," she said.

He regarded her across the table. "What about you? Are you-- I mean, you can tell me if you don't want to answer. Do you want to find another partner?"

She turned towards the window, her finger trailing over the lip of her wineglass. She bit her bottom lip.

He loved how she was thoughtful with her words, not just blurting things out before considering them.

"I honestly don't know. Another partner. There are so many ways to be 'life partners'. And it doesn't have to be romantic. Danny is certainly someone I will spend the rest of my life with.

"But a partnership of love, marriage, forever--it's a choice. Everyday. And continuing to make that choice, choosing that person, that's what makes a soulmate. You can call it fate if you want, but it's really on you. Despite your differences, despite annoyances, you pick them. And I feel like I hit the jackpot once.

"I suppose... I don't believe we only get one chance. But to find it again? How would it be possible for one person to be so lucky?" Her voice caught and her eyes glistened with tears.

Ethan caught her hand. "I didn't mean to make you cry. I'm sorry."

"It's okay. Really," she said. Her voice trembled and she looked up at the ceiling.

He reached his other hand across the table and wiped a tear away with his thumb. "We can change the subject."

"Really, I'm okay. I cry at the drop of a hat."

"I'm a crier, too. Movies, TV, even commercials. Forget it. I'm a fountain," he confessed.

She chortled a bit and dabbed at her eyes with a napkin. "That's very sweet, actually. So, what about you? You said you wanted a partner, but what about marriage? A soulmate?"

He became thoughtful, considering. "Yes," he said without further hesitation. He had, for a long while, pictured himself married with a couple of kids running around. "I do. Definitely."

"I hope you find her," she said, sounding as if she wanted to make sure he knew she wasn't crazy enough to believe that girl could be her.

He looked at her sharply and his heart dropped.

When Evie searched his face, he took a breath, and for the third time in the past day, wondered if what was about to come out of his mouth was wise. Evie seemed to have that effect on him.

"We barely know each other. I totally acknowledge that, because this is real life," he said as he looked deeply into her eyes. "But if I were listing everything I want in a woman, you, so far, have checked off every one."

A nervous look stole over her face. When he saw the effect his words had on her, he took her hand again. "I'm not trying to make you uncomfortable, but you have to know how rare this is for me. How much I'm into you. I know it's a complicated situation. But if you lived here, there isn't a thing in the world that could stop me from trying to be with you.

"Except you, obviously," he finished.

She took a gulp of wine and he watched a flush come over her cheeks. "Listen, Ethan--"

"Don't," he held up a hand to stop her. "I don't want you to say anything. You don't have to say anything."

She arched one eyebrow. "Too bad. I told you not to tell me what to do."

He snorted, remembering their exchange in the elevator. Had that really only been this morning?

"I also fully acknowledge that we don't know each other all that well, and I would like to respond."

As he nodded, giving her the go-ahead, his stomach tightened. He had never, ever laid his feelings on the line like that and was feeling very vulnerable.

She took a deep breath and continued. "Everything has been confusing for me for a long time. I don't know what I want or where my life is going. But something that isn't confusing is the way I feel, deeply, for you. And that's not something I expected to happen. Whatever happens from here on, I'll take it. So… There you go. Do with that what you will."

His whole body relaxed and he brought her hand to his lips. He couldn't stop a wide grin from spreading across his face. Across the table, Evie returned it.

As they ordered and ate their entrees, Ethan felt something solidify between them. Tuesday seemed so far away as she regaled him with tales of her community theatre days. When she laughed at something he said, his soul warmed. He grabbed the bill before she could, eager to continue their evening.

"You paid for breakfast, let me get this," she said.

"Absolutely not. This was my treat."

"Fine, but I get the next one." Her pout was so cute, he leaned all the way over the table and kissed it.

As they left the restaurant, he heard someone say, "What a beautiful couple." He looked down at Evie, eyebrows raised.

"Well, we are. For the next few days, anyway," Evie said.

Ethan frowned and squeezed her closer. "Let's not talk about that."

"It's a pact." They hooked their pinkies together. The night was warm and smelled of late summer flowers as they ambled back to his apartment.

Once back inside, Evie greeted Henry then went out to the balcony. From there, she shot him a look filled with desire.

The anticipation of being with her made Ethan's heart jump in his chest. He selected a John Legend album and played it over his sound system, and then joined her outside. He wrapped his arms around her waist and she rested her head against his chest. A sigh escaped him, and Evie entwined her fingers with his. The lights of Manhattan twinkled at them from across the river. The breeze was warm, but she shivered slightly.

"You cold?" he said.

"The opposite." She turned to him. "This is so fucking romantic."

"Has anyone ever told you that you have a filthy mouth?"

"Wouldn't you like to know?"

A delicious tension hung in the air. He looked into her eyes, matching her every deepening breath.

"Oh, it's on," he growled. Cupping her face in his hands, his mouth captured hers in an eager kiss. She pulled him into the living room by his belt, and he stumbled a bit over a dog toy, nearly toppling Evie. Her laugh was like a windchime and he joined in, while removing his jacket. "I can't even see straight."

"I feel crazed. Like I'm going to explode if you don't take me to bed right now."

He took her by the waist and lifted her easily.

She hooked her legs around him, and pulled her dress over her head.

Every kiss, every touch, set Ethan on fire. He kicked the bedroom door closed and with his lips still on hers, they fell to the bed. She fumbled with his belt buckle. Eager to feel her soft skin on his, he stood and stripped off his t-shirt, then undid his belt.

A sigh escaped her. She lay under his gaze, her face full of passion. "Get over here. Now."

He groaned in impatience and finally kicked aside his jeans. Bending over her, he trailed his tongue down her neck while he pulled her panties off. Propping himself up, he drank in the sight of her creamy skin as she ran her hands over his chest. He met her eyes, and saw in them vulnerability, an openness he hadn't seen before.

"You are so beautiful," he said. "I can't believe I get to see you like this."

"Ethan…" She wrapped her legs around him and pulled him close. "I want you. Please."

"You have no idea."

He felt flustered. He hadn't prepared for such intensity. He moved in her, a tether forming that he knew he wouldn't be able to unknot.

CHAPTER NINE ♫

They lay next to each other, unmoving, breathing hard, their naked bodies soaked in sweat. Evie began to chuckle.

Ethan joined in. When she held her hand up, he met it with a high five, and they laughed harder.

"I mean--" she began. "I mean, I've had some sex…"

"Yeah, same," he said, between chuckles.

"But *that*…"

"Just…"

"I have no words."

"None." He ran a finger down her rib cage towards her hip.

She shuddered.

"Oh god don't. I'm gonna come again," she said breathlessly.

"I, however, am going to need a minute." He propped his head on one elbow and looked down at her. "Seriously, that was fucking fantastic."

"I had a feeling it would be."

"Same here," he said.

"But I was not expecting…you know." She bit her lip.

"The intensity?" He thought she felt it too, the way she looked at him when he was inside her, as if she couldn't get close enough.

"Exactly. I guess I...really like you, Ethan." She stroked the side of his face. He brushed her hair off of her cheek and they gazed at each other for a long moment. "And what was that thing you did with your hips? That was amazing."

"Oh no, that thing you did when you arched back? I thought I was going to die of pleasure," Ethan said. He looked into her face, flushed and happy, and kissed her softly. "This is the most infatuated I have been since, like, high school."

"God, same. The last time I felt this way--" Her eyebrows knitted together and she frowned slightly.

Even though he could see her in his life, he didn't want to pressure her to feel anything she wasn't ready for. He gently squeezed her hand. "This is a very good fling."

"I concur." Evie curled her body into his. He put his arms around her, and they stayed that way for a few wonderful minutes, while Evie's hand traveled the length of his torso, and his fingers tickled the freckles on her shoulder.

"Are you thirsty?" he said after a while.

"After that, I should say so." She stretched, clearly satisfied.

He got up and grabbed his phone, intending to head to the kitchen.

At the doorway, he turned back, reluctant to let her out of his sight. He watched Evie sit up, facing away from the door, with the moonlight backlighting her.

Ethan stared at her sexy bare back for a moment, counting himself incredibly lucky.

Several notifications greeted him on his homescreen: friends confirming a basketball game he was supposed to play the next morning. After considering for a minute, he sent a response.

> Sorry guys, I think I'm going to have to cancel just this once. I kind of met someone.

A flurry of texts followed, all astonished, wanting to know who she was.

> She's only here until Tuesday. Calm down. I'll catch you guys next week.

Emojis, most in poor taste, followed his cancellation. He chuckled, locked his phone, and poured two glasses of water, all the while smiling to himself.

Once she was alone, Evie typed to Daniel.

> Oh honey. Perfection. Absolutely perfection. Be jealous. How's Max?

> YAAAAAS I am so glad to hear it. Max is a delight. We're headed for a drink. Have fun babe. Don't do anything I wouldn't do.

> Which isn't much. Say goodnight, Evie.

> Goodnight, Evie.

She turned when Ethan came back to the bed and handed her a glass of water.

"So," Ethan said, "round two?"

Evie straddled him. "Put me in, coach," she said.

He groaned and kissed her fiercely. "You are perfect."

§

Evie opened her eyes and saw sunlight spilling into the room. Henry was sitting on the floor, staring right at her. "Hey," she said, "creepy."

89

She rolled over. The clock said 8:35. Ethan was splayed over the bed, on his stomach, sleeping soundly. Warmth filled her heart as she played back the events of the evening. She'd wondered if the passion she felt was fueled by the wine or his fame. But the connection she felt this morning seemed even stronger. She could be real with him, could tell him things that would make other partners uncomfortable. Being with him was easy--it was almost familiar.

She ran a hand through his hair and he mumbled something in his sleep.

Henry whined.

"You wanna go for a walk, buddy?"

He stood, wagging his tail.

"You are too cute." She got out of bed and, after brushing her teeth, took Henry outside.

When she returned to the apartment twenty minutes later, she found Ethan, wearing only boxer briefs, making coffee. She stepped up behind him and put her arms around his waist. "Morning."

He added nutmeg to the grounds. "For a second I thought you stole my dog and ran."

She looked over at Henry, who was currently rolling around in a patch of sunshine in the most adorable way. "Don't rule it out."

He turned, her arms still around him, and kissed her warmly.

"Aww, you brushed your teeth."

"Morning breath is my one flaw."

"I knew there had to be something."

"So last night was…" he began, distinct pleasure in his voice.

"Something else, man."

"No kidding. Wanna know something?"

"Ooh…an intrigue!"

"I was supposed to play basketball today. For the first time ever, I cancelled."

She felt a little twinge of guilt. "No way. You didn't have to do that. You should have gone."

"Please," he said and rolled his eyes. "That show you put on last night made me forget about it entirely."

"Well thank you, good sir. I'm ever so flattered." It was her turn to be lady of the manor.

"Yes, quite. Quite good."

"If there is anything I can do for you, do let me know. Our servants are here at your disposal." She bowed deeply, which seemed to amuse him.

Straightening up, she saw a serious look cross his face, something like longing. Her gaze met his and her heart began to race. "What is it?"

He grasped her hand, pulling her closer. "I'm not ready for Tuesday."

"Tuesday is ages away."

He traced her lips with his thumb and then kissed her hungrily. Evie felt an invisible tether between them, pulling her toward him in a way she couldn't describe. What she thought she wanted was sex with a hot Broadway star. But this was more than that, deeper and unexpected.

He lifted her onto the counter, his eyes alight with desire.

Greedily, she drew him closer. Just kissing him set her body on fire.

After a passionate few minutes, she rested her forehead against his, breathing heavily.

How could one person in such a short time make her feel so wanted?

"Evie. My god. You are a dream."

What did this connection mean when the relationship couldn't go anywhere?

"Ethan, I'm..."

"Yes?" His expression was hopeful.

"I'm..." She wasn't sure what exactly she was going to say, but she knew she wasn't ready to say it. "...caffeine-deprived."

A look of disappointment crossed his face but disappeared immediately. "Of course." He poured her a cup of coffee.

"Thank you," She hopped off the counter and accepted it, her fingers brushing his. Peripherally, she saw his phone lighting up with messages. "Your buddies?"

"They're trying to make me jealous." Ethan scrolled through the photos of his friends on the basketball court. "Little do they know, I'm having the time of my life."

"I'm a bit skeptical of that. I'm just some gal you met. You've been in a movie with Meryl Streep."

"I was in one scene and she wasn't on set the day I shot it. Trust me, this is better."

"You've been onstage with Patti Lupone. *Patti Lupone.*"

"Okay, I admit, that was pretty awe-inspiring."

"See?"

Ethan enveloped her in his arms. "But with you? With you..." He started to sing. "...everything's coming up roses."

A snicker escaped her before she could stop it, and she could see the laughter in Ethan's eyes. "Oh my god, now who's the cheeseball."

Her coffee abandoned, she let him lead her in a dance to the shower while he belted out Patti Lupone's infamous song from *Gypsy*.

§

After a scrambled egg breakfast on the balcony, Ethan wrapped his arms around her as they gazed at the street below. The day was warm, and a lazy Sunday morning played out before them. Strollers were pushed by mothers juggling bags and sippy cups, couples walked hand in hand to brunch. Evie gave a contented sigh.

"What do you want to do today?" she said. She watched a teenager bounce a basketball up the sidewalk.

"I was thinking we could take Henry to the park. Have a picnic. But before that, if it's okay with you, I wanted to hit the gym."

"Actually, that's great. I need to put in my headphones and just walk for like two hours." When he looked at her quizzically, she shrugged. "It's my thing. Gotta disappear into my head. The introverted side of me needs to be alone for a bit."

"Perfect, mine too. Let's do that," Ethan said. He lowered his lips to her neck and she shivered.

She felt palpably how compatible they were.

Downstairs, Ethan handed her a spare set of keys. She glanced around the street. No one was paying attention, so she kissed him quickly.

"Have a good walk, Freckles." He brushed his hand against the side of her face and turned to go. She watched him walk away for a few pensive moments, then turned and went in the opposite direction.

Evie turned her music to shuffle and wandered around Brooklyn, thinking not about Ethan, but Liam. Her playlist included all the songs that made her think of him. She envisioned his curly brown hair, his warm brown eyes framed by dark eyelashes. She remembered the way he made her laugh. The way he called her "sweet thing." The night he'd proposed. Their wedding day.

The way on their first date he had said one of the first things that Ethan had: "*Should we just get married?*"

She barely noticed where she was going as her feet slapped the pavement, and she didn't particularly care. Her eyes started to burn, and she began to cry. She cried for what she'd lost, and she cried for what she'd never get to have with Liam. The tears streaked freely down her face and she let them. She didn't care how ridiculous she looked. She needed to feel cleansed.

On a corner, she stood at the window of a bakery. As she looked at the pastries and cakes that Liam would have loved, a chuckle almost escaped her. She remembered some of his last words to her.

"More than cake and brownies and even pie."

She turned away from the bakery and took deep breaths. She wiped her eyes and felt the residual guilt ease.

I love you, Liam. But I'm moving on. Probably not with Ethan, but with my life. You were everything to me for so long, and I have to move forward or I'm going to be stuck forever. I hope you understand, wherever you are. You were the best husband.

Feeling cleansed, she glanced at her phone.

Three hours had passed. Ethan had texted twice, worried about where she was. She felt frantic after her moment of calm and she raced back to his apartment.

§

As Ethan worked out, he thought about the situation he was in. It was a real-life romantic comedy. A tragic heroine. A handsome hero. And while the sex was mind-blowing, the best part was that, Evie was a whole person. As funny as she was kind, as dorky as she was sexy. She didn't seem to need his validation; it all came from within. And even if their affair was short lived and complicated, he was giddy that it was happening. *Maybe this is enough,* he thought, and smiled to himself.

Three hours later, he sat on the couch only half paying attention to the news. He flipped the remote over and over in his hand, glancing at his phone every other second. He set down the remote, picked up his phone and began to type. Before he pressed send, he put it back down. Drumming his fingers on his knee, he considered that she had just taken off. But why would she leave all of her stuff?

Where was she?

Finally, he heard a key in the lock and bolted up. At the sight of her, relief flooded through him. Then he noticed that her face was flushed, her eyes teary.

He gently tipped her chin up to him, full of concern.

"I'm sorry I'm late," she said, her voice wavering.

"You've been crying."

She closed her eyes and shook her head, but it didn't seem defiant. It was as if she needed to shake something loose. "I had to think about some stuff."

Tenderly, he wrapped his arms around her and gathered her to his chest. He felt her breathe shakily when he buried his face in her hair. Moments passed and he felt her breathing grow steady.

"Do you want to talk?" She eased back and put a hand on his chest, her eyes clear and bright.

"No. No, I'm okay." She rose onto tiptoes and pressed her lips gently to his.

"Wanna take Henry to the park?"

"Definitely."

CHAPTER TEN ♫

They walked to the park near his building, armed with a blanket, snacks, and drinks from the nearby bodega. Henry's Frisbee and balls were in a bag on Ethan's back. After spreading the blanket under a tree in the park, he let Henry off-leash. He tossed a ball for the dog as Evie readied their bread and cheese, veggies, and fresh fruits. It was a gorgeous Sunday afternoon, and the park was packed. Ethan was wearing a hat and sunglasses, although Evie thought his smile and physique made him easy to spot if you knew what to look for.

She ripped off a piece of baguette and smeared it with a good amount of goat cheese. After popping it in her mouth, she hummed with delight.

Ethan watched her with affection. He moved to touch her but stopped suddenly.

Evie swallowed. "Something wrong? Is it my obvious love of cheese? I can't help it, I'm Midwestern. It's in my genes."

He snickered. "No, that's understandable. I just think it's wise to keep our distance in public, just in case. I don't want you to have to deal with my internet savvy fans. They're like detectives. If your picture is on the internet, they will somehow find out everything about you."

Evie glanced around, uneasy at the thought of strangers hunting for information about her. All of her social media was private, but there were various items about her non-profit work. What really concerned her were the articles written after Liam's death. She adjusted her sunglasses. "I definitely don't want that."

"Good thing we're just pals."

She slugged him playfully in the shoulder. "Good buddies."

"Friends to the end. Like Marius and Enjolras."

"Is *Les Misérables* really what we want to balance this 'friendship' on?"

"Until the French Revolution begins, sure." He tossed a baby carrot into his mouth and grinned.

After they'd eaten, and it was clear that no one was paying attention to them, Evie started tossing Henry the Frisbee, while Ethan, still lying on the blanket, took an occasional photo. The game went on for nearly a quarter of an hour before Henry finally lost interest and rolled on the grass, panting. Ethan was reaching for dog treats when she noticed the three girls standing on the nearby path.

They were blatantly staring. At Ethan.

"Shit," Evie said, "I didn't see them."

He casually followed her gaze. The girls were clearly trying to be cool about raising phones in their direction.

Unnerved, Evie began to pack up the food.

"Man. This rarely happens in New York. Let's just hang out for a bit, and I'll let Julie know."

The tension in his face was obvious, though he was trying to hide it. She looked over his shoulder as he quickly typed a text to his publicist.

Jules, chicks in the park snapping photos of Evie and Henry and me. Not sure how long they've been watching, just noticed them. Just FYI, social media will probably blow up in a second.

A few minutes later, his phone buzzed.

Well. She's very pretty. :) Don't worry, it's total speculation, and it's just photos of her and the dog with you in the background. Under control.

When Ethan sighed, Evie bit her lip, sorry she'd complicated things.

The tension drained from his face. "Hey," he said, "don't look like that. It's no big deal, okay?"

"Okay, fine. But, since we've been outed, why don't we pick up food for dinner tonight instead of going out?"

"An excellent idea," he said, and began packing up Henry's things. "Henry. To me." The dog trotted over.

The girls were still pointing phones their way.

"God, that's fucking obnoxious," Evie said.

Ethan looked at her wryly. "Double edged sword. I'm so grateful for their love and support. Obviously, I wouldn't have a career without them. And I love to meet fans after shows or at the stage door. But this kind of thing…they don't warn you about it. It makes me feel so exposed.

At least it doesn't happen that often. Honestly, I wish they would just come say hi. That would be way less intrusive." He rubbed his hand over his chin, clearly still frustrated.

Evie almost instinctively reached for his hand and stopped herself just in time. "Oops."

His eyes were hidden behind his sunglasses, but a small smile formed on his lips. "Let's get out of here." At the park's exit, she watched Ethan glance furtively around. No girls, no phones. Thank goodness. They maintained a safe distance from each other as they walked back to his building.

Outside of the bodega, Evie waited with Henry while Ethan bought groceries for dinner. Back at the apartment, he loaded the perishables in the fridge and turned to look at her. "What should we do now? Too early to make dinner."

A grin spread slowly across her face and she began to walk backwards towards the bedroom. He hastened after her, stripping off his clothes as he went.

§

Evie opened one eye and peered through tangled hair at the bedside clock. She'd slept nearly two hours. Ethan's arm was draped over her and he was gently snoring against her neck. Her stomach growled. She rolled over and nipped his neck.

Before opening his eyes, he smiled and pulled her closer. His lips found hers and he kissed her tenderly. "I could get used to this."

She snuggled closer. "Me too. You hungry?"

"Ravenous." He stood and headed to the bathroom.

"Hey. I like the view," she said to his bare ass.

He turned and winked at her, gave her naked body a full once-over, and then raised his hands to mime taking a photo. "Ditto, gorgeous."

Evie got up and pulled a sleeveless swing dress from her bag. She pulled it on, enjoying the soft cotton against her skin.

Setting water on a burner to boil, she moved about the kitchen, beginning dinner preparations.

Ethan emerged in the bedroom doorway, a pair of black sweatpants sexily hanging on his hips, a white t-shirt in his hand, his chest bare.

"Can I help you?" she said.

He smiled his crooked smile. "Oh no, please, I'm enjoying the view of you making me dinner."

She gave him a blank stare and a Stepford smile, before pulling the largest knife from his set. Robotically, she sliced the lemons. "Anything for you, my love," she said through her teeth.

"You're a goddamn creep," he said affectionately.

"Thank you," she said, accepting that as a compliment.

After starting his Motown playlist, he joined her in the kitchen to prepare their meal. Each task she performed was complemented by what he did, as if choreographed. They danced around each other. When Ethan went to the balcony to put the salmon on the grill, she took a sip of the dry Chardonnay he'd poured. She watched him through the window, a hand over her heart.

§

Midway through their salmon, Ethan remembered the Broadway Cares gala. He thought the situation through. His connection to Evie was on the internet already. If Paige was still keeping tabs on him and saw the photos, she would probably think he was just hiding Evie like he'd hid her. That certainly wasn't the case. And while he wanted to protect Evie, she didn't have to agree to have her picture taken or to give her name to any photographers.

He looked at the beautiful redhead over the candles he'd lit and felt full to bursting. He wanted to shout her name from the rooftops.

Evie looked at him expectantly, her eyes bright green in the candlelight.

He sat forward, steepling his palms in front of his mouth.

She glanced around impatiently as he kept gazing at her, contemplative. "Oh my god, what, you weirdo?"

He burst out laughing.

She folded her arms. "Okay, I'll wait."

"I just adore you, that's all. I also have a proposition for you."

"Ooh, am I getting paid for all of this?"

He rolled his eyes. "Shut up and listen. There's this gala tomorrow night. It's Broadway Cares/Equity Fights AIDS

100

biggest benefit of the year. I'm going, and I'd like you to come. If you want to. There will be press, but you can avoid it pretty easily."

"Okay. So... A party with a bunch of my Broadway heroes? Why are you saying this like it would be pulling teeth for me?"

"Well. Because also--" He took a deep breath. "--my ex will be there."

"Okay." Evie was clearly not seeing the problem.

"And she's... Well, she doesn't like me."

"Okay."

"And she will *really* hate you."

Evie sighed, took her last bite of salmon, and chewed slowly. "Okay. Why don't you tell me what happened between you?"

He echoed her sigh and took a swig of wine. Reluctantly, he described the desperation Paige felt to go public about their relationship, the week of radio silence, and her unexpected visit.

When he got to the naked break up, and his calling her a crazy bitch and slamming the door in her face, Evie chortled. "Yeah, that's pretty bad. I've had worse, but that's pretty bad."

Avoiding her eyes, he grimaced. "You think I'm terrible now, don't you?"

Evie shrugged and narrowed her eyes at him. She sat forward.

"I once walked out on a guy when he got up to pee during sex because I was bored."

"Evie..."

"I once told a guy he was too tall for me and never took another call from him again. That was it. We had dated for eight months."

"Evelyn," he said, now a warning.

"I once broke up with a guy by straight up telling him I wanted to sleep with another guy. Not that I wanted to 'see other people', literally another specific guy. Which I then

101

did, by the way." She took a swig of wine, one eyebrow raised.

"I get it," he said, unable to resist smiling at her.

"We all do shitty things. It happens." She shrugged again and returned his grin.

"Paige is special," Ethan insisted.

"No, she's not. She's a woman who got her feelings hurt. I can handle it."

Ethan regarded Evie across the table. He couldn't remember meeting a more self-assured person in his life. "So, you'll come with me then?"

"Try and stop me." She raised her glass.

As they dried the last of the dishes, Evie looked over at the piano. "Do you play?"

"Not very well. Enough to prep myself for a performance and warm up, but that's it."

She looked at him, then nodded at the piano. "Get over there."

He laughed and turned off the dinner music. Taking her hand, he led her to the piano, where he pulled out the bench which was just the right size to seat them close together. After kissing her slow and deep, he opened a binder of sheet music and flipped to the song he wanted.

She listened to him play for a few bars, and then said, "Not very well my ass."

He began to sing "You Matter To Me" from *Waitress: The Musical*, his beautiful tenor filling the loft.

Evie closed her eyes, relishing Ethan's voice so close to her.

She knew the tune, and it was a duet. Eyes still closed, she sang the second verse.

"I didn't know you could sing like that," he said as he continued to play.

"You didn't ask. I'm no Ethan Carter, but I can hang."

"You're full of surprises."

"So are you, Carter." She kissed him, and then finished the song in harmony with him.

When the duet was finished, silence fell. Evie's heart raced. She gazed into Ethan's eyes for a moment, seeing there the hunger she felt. She kissed him deeply. He pulled her toward him until she straddled him on the bench. Evie found the silence exquisite, the last sweet note they sang together lingering in the air.

She felt his breath on her neck, felt his breathing deepen.

A desperation filled her. She needed to be closer to him. Gazing into his eyes, she slid onto him and he gripped her waist. She found she couldn't break eye contact with him, their breathing increasing as they moved passionately together, their bodies intertwined and burning.

"Evie," he gasped. She wound her fingers through his hair.

They came together, moaning, still staring deeply into each other's eyes.

"Ho...ly..." Ethan said, when they stilled.

Evie gaped at him, only able to nod. She collapsed onto him, spent, and nestled her face into his neck.

He sighed contentedly and ran a hand down her back.

"That was incredible," she said.

"That might be the most intense sex I have ever had."

"Seriously."

"I need to lie down."

"Me too. I'm shaking."

Gently, he helped her stand and they made their way to the bed. They collapsed and snuggled down under the covers.

"This is just...marvelous," she said and looked up at him, at his clear blue eyes, at the small smile playing on his lips. She felt a jolt in her heart so strong it was almost painful.

Ethan looked into Evie's shining face and thought about what had just taken place. He hadn't lied. That really had been the most intense sex he'd ever had. His heart beat faster at the thought of her, not just naked and on top of him, but laughing in the sunlight and cooking in his kitchen, snuggling with Henry, and he was warmed at the memory of her kindness to everyone they had met in the past two days.

This woman astonished him. She felt new and familiar all at once, and he let the part of himself that was just hovering on the edge go free, let himself fall for her completely. He kissed her and relished a few more minutes with the warmth of her body next to his.

"I hate to say this, but I have to go back to the real world for a bit. I have an audition later this week I need to prepare for. Is that okay?"

"Of course. Can you tell me what it's for?" She got up and went to get her book from her bag.

He reached for his laptop and glasses on the bedside table and pulled up the audition materials. "All I can say is it's a Netflix series."

"That's so exciting. What's the part?"

He grinned at her. "That's all I can tell you, for now."

"Fair enough." She shrugged and opened her book. She read intently, her facial expressions changing as she reacted to the story. He couldn't make himself look away from her. After a minute or so, she smiled slowly, while still looking at her book. "You're not going to get very far if you just keep watching me read."

"Can't help it."

"You're a dream come true, you know that?" she said.

That frankness again. Ethan smiled and turned to his laptop. "You have no idea."

A few minutes later Henry trotted in and whined. Ethan, deeply engrossed in his work, sighed at the thought of having to get up.

Before he could move, Evie hopped up, and went to the closet "Don't worry about it, I'll take him."

Ethan stared as she zipped his hoodie over her dress and slipped on her Chucks. "Who *are* you?" he wondered aloud.

She walked over and kissed his cheek. "Go get 'em, tiger," she said and tapped the screen. She left with the dog.

Ethan was left to concentrate on his work, which he found easy, knowing Henry was in such good hands.

He felt something coming. Something good.

CHAPTER ELEVEN ♫

"Okay. Well. So, you're totally falling for him." Evie was talking to Daniel as she walked Henry up the block. She had just given him a rundown of the day's events--the park, the gala invite, the duet--after which he'd been silent for a full minute.

"I am not *falling* for him. But this is super intense," Evie said.

"Evelyn. You *sang* a *duet*. You are in a literal musical." Daniel had a smile in his voice.

Evie snorted. "How's Max?"

Daniel sighed. "Oh, a dream, obviously. He's a lovely man. We had wonderful time Saturday night. Going to see each other tomorrow...after my callback for *Fully Engaged*."

Evie jumped up and down. "Really?" she squealed.

"Yep. It's happening. If this goes well, I'll have to come back in like a month or something to go in front of the producers and read with the rest of the cast."

"Daniel! It's all happening."

"I know."

"Amazing," Evie said, overjoyed.

"Hey, why don't you and Ethan come to dinner tomorrow night with Max and me?"

"That sounds great. Would you be interested in coming to the gala with us afterwards?" Evie said.

"I would love to. You know how much I love Broadway Cares."

"I'll run it by him. Text me the dinner details when you have them."

"I will. And Evie?"

"Yeah?"

"It's wonderful to hear you so happy."

"Love you, Danny."

"Love you. Goodnight."

Evie pocketed her phone as Henry tugged her back toward Ethan's building.

Ethan had printed out his scenes for the audition and was pacing the bedroom as he read over the monologue. The apartment door opened. He watched as Evie gave Henry a treat, then joined her in the kitchen.

"Hey, glasses," she said.

"Hey, Freckles."

"I just talked to Daniel. He wants us to have dinner with him and Max tomorrow. And I thought maybe they could come with us to the gala. Is that possible?"

"Absolutely, I'll email Julie and get them on the list."

"Perfect. They're having a fling too."

"And we'll have a double date."

"Does a fling involve 'dates', *per se*?"

"Don't be pedantic," he scolded. He wrapped his arms around her.

"Me? Never."

Propping his chin on the top of her head, he sighed deeply. "Tell me Tuesday doesn't exist."

She wrapped her arms around his waist and turned her face up to him, a wistful look in her eyes. "Tuesday? Never heard of it."

§

Ethan rolled over, hearing Henry pawing at the bedroom door. "Buddy," he moaned, "do shut up."

Henry yipped and ran to the bed, and then back to the bedroom door.

Ethan sat up and looked at the clock. Ten-fifteen. "Oh no. Sorry, dude." He quickly hopped out of bed and dressed, while Henry waited expectantly by the front door.

"Make it quick, buddy, that beautiful woman is only here for one more day," he said as he closed the door behind them.

Upon his return, he fed Henry and started the coffee. His heart full at the sight of Evie in his bed, he watched her stir and stretch. He went into the bedroom and sat beside her. "Morning, Freckles."

She smiled dreamily at him. "Hey. We slept in."

"We did. We've been pretty active the past couple of days."

She held out her arms.

He nuzzled his face into her warm neck.

"My thighs will never be the same," she murmured.

"Neither will my abs."

"Sex is such a good workout."

"Mmmf," he moaned. He lifted his head and searched her lovely face, growing a little sad. "Evie..."

She put a finger against his lips and shook her head. "We have about thirty-six more hours. Let's make the most of it."

Two nights ago, he'd told her she was everything he was looking for. All he could do was have faith that she knew how he felt. For the moment, he decided to let this conversation go.

"I've got to get a dress for the gala tonight," Evie said later over coffee and toast.

"Sounds good. I wanted to hit the gym again. But I'll go shopping with you if you want."

"I don't drag men shopping. It'll be boring." She stood and picked up her bag and his spare keys. He followed her to the door.

"I like shopping."

"For yourself."

"Well...yeah," he said, "but now it's only thirty-five hours."

A gloomy expression on her face, she stood on her tiptoes, and kissed him. "I'm a quick shopper. I'll see you later, Carter." She left him standing there, feeling the weight of her departure the next day on his shoulders.

§

After a long workout at the gym, Ethan showered while his thoughts raced. How was he going to say goodbye to this incredible woman?

He was dressed and ready to head home when his phone sounded. He looked at the screen and narrowed his eyes, seeing that the message was from a contact he'd labeled *DO NOT RESPOND*.

Paige. What the hell, why now?

His heart hammered. He didn't want to deal with Paige on top of all of his feelings for Evie. But knowing he would never stop wondering what it said if he didn't, he opened the text sent twenty minutes ago.

So I guess you've moved on then.

Of course. She would have seen the photos of Evie in the park. And fifteen minutes ago:

Wish you weren't such an asshole. Then I might be happy for you.

And just now.

I knew you wouldn't respond. Coward.

The gall of her. He deleted the texts and left the gym, fuming.

Evie could tell that something was off when she returned with a garment bag draped across her arm. She looked at him questioningly. He shook his head, draped the garment bag over a chair, and wrapped her in a hug.

"What's up?" she asked. She saw his jaw was clenched.

"Fucking...Paige texted me. She saw your photo. I know I was horrible to her, but she's just mean.

"She's mean," he repeated, his voice low and sad.

Evie surprised herself by seeing red. She knew she felt deeply for him, but this kind of rage was usually reserved for people like Daniel, whom she would protect fiercely. Ethan sounded so hurt that all she wanted to do was punch this bitch in the face. She shoved away from him. "I want to kill her for making you look and sound like that."

Ethan arched an eyebrow. "You're a little scary," he said. He seemed flattered by her outrage.

"I don't like it when jerks hurt the people I care about." She clenched both hands into tight fists.

He held up his hands, palms out. "Hey, whoa, it's okay. I'm fine. I'm over it. And honestly, can't wait to show you off tonight."

Evie forced her fists to relax and the burning fire she felt to settle. "Sorry."

He laughed and wrapped her in his arms again. "'And though she be but little, she is fierce.' Remind me never to cross you."

She smiled into his chest. "I can't help it. I'm Irish." Winding her fingers in his hair, she kissed him, feeling the remnants of her anger subside.

"So, you're still okay with going tonight?" He searched her face.

"I am, but also wonder if it is wise. I mean...this can't...it isn't..."

He tilted his head, obviously wondering what she was stuttering about.

Evie took a deep breath. "This thing between us isn't going to go anywhere. So why even bother if it's just going to create drama for you?"

His expression softened and he bent his head to her, brushing her nose with his. "I, for some reason, don't care about the rumors. Let them come."

"That's quite a change of tune," she said while eyeing him suspiciously.

"Maybe it's because it can't go anywhere, that I don't mind?"

She tilted her head at him and decided to accept his reasoning. "Well then, let's party it up, my friend."

§

The rest of the afternoon passed quickly as they lounged and laughed in bed, loving on each other. Ethan was beginning to see life after Tuesday dimly, the color sapped out of it.

"We should probably get ready for the party, don't you think?" Evie said. She sat up and combed her fingers through her snarled hair, frowning.

"You could go looking just like that and you'd still be the most beautiful woman in the room."

Evie looked down at herself then met his eyes. "I'm naked, Ethan."

He grinned widely and shrugged. "And?"

She threw a pillow at him and got out of bed to get ready. "Wait till you see this dress."

At the door, she turned, looking contemplative.

"Yes?"

"Life in Chicago is going to be so different after this weekend." She walked away and that simple sentence reverberated in his mind as he dressed.

Ethan straightened his collar in a mirror on the wall, anticipating the evening ahead. His first public date in years, and the only thing he felt nervous about was seeing Paige face-to-face for the first time since the break-up.

111

In the mirror, Evie appeared behind him in a red chiffon dress that brushed the floor. He turned, stilled by her beauty. The straps crossed her chest and tied behind her neck. She had gathered her auburn hair in a loose, stylish knot on the top of her head.

She turned around slowly, revealing that the dress swooped low and her back was bare.

"My word, you are a goddess."

"You sure?" She pulled up the bottom of the dress, revealing her black Chucks.

He put his hands in his pockets and chuckled. "Absolutely, one-hundred percent, Grade-A goddess."

She beamed at him. "Damn Carter, you can wear a suit."

He spun and strutted the length of the room. "Dior does a body good," he said. He offered his hand. "Shall we, my lady?"

"Indeed, my lord."

As they rode to Manhattan in a town car sent by Ethan's agency, Ethan said, "Just so you know, we'll be in Midtown. I might get recognized."

Evie shrugged. "I'll make myself scarce, don't worry." Her wry smile made it clear she understood the delicateness of the situation.

"You don't have to do that--"

She had laid one finger across his lips. "Buddy, I understand. Don't worry about me."

He dropped his forehead to hers. "I can't even tell you what that means to me."

Indeed, a few heads did turn at Ethan's appearance when they walked into the restaurant. A modern bar stood in the middle of the room, contrasting with the eclectic collection of French country chairs and tables. The navy blue walls were adorned with gold framed art; modern gold light fixtures hung from the ceiling. As the host led them to their table, Ethan watched Evie take in the buzz of obvious comments that followed in their path. Her shoulders had tightened. He placed a hand on the small of her back, wanting her to feel at ease. Happily, no one approached for a selfie.

Daniel and Max waved from the table they'd already secured.

Max stood and kissed Evie's cheek as Daniel and Ethan hugged. "My good goddess, you two are the most attractive people I have ever seen."

"It is wildly inappropriate how pretty the two of you are," Daniel concurred.

"Well, thank you. And talk about handsome. Look at these suits. You look great, boys." Evie said as they took their seats. She and Ethan settled their napkins in their lap and ordered drinks from the server. All the while Daniel and Max were staring at them like goons, huge smiles on their faces.

"What?" Evie said.

"It's just that Ethan is totally smitten with you and I'm loving it," Max said.

Daniel nodded his agreement. "And I haven't seen you this happy in a long time."

Ethan reached for Evie's hand under the table and squeezed it.

"We're having a great time together. For the next twenty-four hours," Evie said.

Ethan groaned and rolled his eyes. "You have *got* to stop doing that."

"I can't believe I have to say this again, but don't tell me what to do," she challenged, as they glared at each other.

"I'll do what I want," Ethan said fiercely, his intense gaze holding hers.

"Oh my god," Max blurted, "can you imagine what they're like in bed?" Ethan and Daniel laughed along with Evie. While they drank their aperitifs, they talked about what Daniel and Max were up to, and how well Daniel's callback had gone. After they ordered entrees, Evie excused herself.

Daniel gave Ethan a hard stare, once Evie was safely out of earshot. Ethan braced himself a bit, knowing what was coming.

"Listen, Ethan--"

"You don't have to give me the 'don't hurt her' bit. A) I wouldn't and B) this is just a fling," he said.

Daniel's expression softened. "That's not what I was going to say. What I want to tell you is: that woman is the most incredible human I know. For ten years, I've called her Evie "First Responder" O'Hara. She is the first on the scene of a breakup. She's in the front row of every show, and she's the first to bring over a bottle of wine when you're feeling down. She will drop everything to help her friends in need. Not just for me, but for all of us. She gives the best advice but won't push you to take it. She has never, not once, said she would do something and not done it. She is the most fiercely loyal, independent, generous person I know, and you should be so lucky to be with her.

"And from what I can see of you two, and from what Max says about you, you deserve her. So, if this is something you want, I'm certain you can convince her to give it a go. Either way, you'll have a friend for life in Evie."

When he'd finished, Ethan found he couldn't speak for several moments. He cleared his throat.

Max sent him a sympathetic look.

"Honestly, Daniel, the thought of her leaving tomorrow makes me sick to my stomach," he said. "Everything after tomorrow has lost its color. If I could..." But he stopped when he saw Evie approaching. Once she was seated, he put his arm around her shoulders and kissed her temple, and then excused himself.

She watched him walk away and then gave Daniel a pointed look. "What did you do?"

"Nothing. I simply told him he should be so lucky to be with you," Daniel said.

Evie arched a brow.

Max cleared his throat. "I feel like I should say something here."

114

Daniel and Evie turned his way.

"You should be so lucky, too, Evie. I mean, Ethan is a wonderful man. He's not only everything you already know about him, he's incredibly genuine, and romantic, and he loves so fiercely and with such gratitude…"

"I know, Max. But it's complicated." Evie reached across to take his hand.

He caught hers and squeezed it gently. "I know it is honey, but even we can feel how right you are for each other."

"I…"

"Just don't rule it out." He looked into her eyes, his expression earnest.

She gave him a soft smile. "I will try not to," she said with finality.

Daniel had an adoring look on his face. He gave Max a kiss on the cheek.

Evie sat back. "And I know Daniel probably waxed poetic about me--"

Daniel held his hands up. "It is my duty, darling."

"So, just so you know, Max, Daniel is a perfect human who can do no wrong."

"I'm beginning to see that," Max said. He took Daniel's hand.

"But seriously. He saved my life and he's the best friend I've ever had. You're very lucky."

"Are we just going to sit around saying how lucky we are this whole dinner?" Ethan had returned.

As he sat back down, Max raised his glass to each of them in turn. "To us, some really lucky S-O-Bs."

§

As the town car approached the Manhattan Center, Evie felt her stomach flutter. She could see NYPD barriers set up in front of the venue. Dozens of fans stood behind them and held out old Playbills for autographs. She felt Ethan inhale deeply.

"Hey Sam, can you drive around the block?" he said. He picked at the cuff of his sleeve as they drove past the cheering crowd.

Evie put a hand on his arm. "So how are we going to work this?"

He straightened his pocket square. "Max, you take them in the door furthest from the barriers. I'll walk the crowd and meet you inside. Would you mind getting out up the block and walking?"

"Not at all," Max said. Daniel and Evie nodded their agreement.

"Excellent. Sam, drop them off on the corner of 9th and 34th. Then could you bring me to the front?"

"Sure thing, boss."

"Ooh, boss. I like that." Evie tried to flirt, but she could see the tautness of his jaw. "Hey, if this is too much for you, I don't have to go in."

He closed his eyes and drew her close. "No way. I want you there. I'm just a little nervous, that's all."

The car stopped and Max and Daniel exited. Ethan held onto Evie for a moment and kissed her gently. "I'll see you in there, Freckles."

"Go get 'em, tiger." She squeezed his hand. Daniel helped her out of the car and waved to Ethan.

Straightening her dress, she turned toward the venue which was abuzz with excitement. Guests in glittering gowns and outlandish suits were being led inside. Further on, in front of the barriers, she noticed the star of the hottest show open. Fans clamored for the chance of a selfie with her. The butterflies in Evie's stomach intensified--all of her favorite Broadway stars, mere steps away. The Empire State Building glittered in the distance. She threaded her arm through Daniel's and beamed up at him.

Max took Daniel's other arm. "Off to see the wizard?"

Daniel glanced at Evie. "I don't think we're in Kansas anymore."

She bounced on her feet and gave off a little squeal. "Let's do this, Scarecrow."

Max led them to the line and gave their names to the bouncer. Inside the grand foyer, there was a scrum of photographers and media centered in front of a step-and-repeat bearing the Broadway Cares logo. Evie's stomach tightened at the thought of getting her picture taken.

"I'm going to hang back, but you guys go ahead."

"So this is what almost-famous feels like." Daniel raised his eyebrows at Evie as Max led him away. She watched as Daniel and Max posed for the cameras and smiled quietly to herself. Outside, a massive cheer erupted. She was certain that was the signal that Ethan had arrived.

Done with their moment in the spotlight, Max and Daniel escorted her into the ballroom. "Ethan is going to be a while with the fans and the media. I saw that guy from OMGCeleb. He's a notorious gossip and wants the dirt on everyone. Ethan can't stand--" Max seemed to realize she wasn't listening.

Evie knew her mouth was agape and she didn't care. Amber and red spotlights shone down on dozens of cocktail tables in the massive ballroom. The largest chandelier Evie had ever seen hung above the floor and around it, she could see three levels of balconies. A stage stood towards the front of the room, the gold curtain closed. She wandered down a small flight of stairs and touched the purple zinnias on one of the table arrangements. This ballroom, this gala, this weekend-- She felt like Sleeping Beauty, finally awake.

Daniel's gentle hand on her arm pulled her out of her trance. He stood beside Max, his eyes wide. "Is this real life? Are we really here right now?"

"I honestly don't know."

"I am going to lose it, maybe."

"Stay cool, boy!" she said.

"Evelyn, you can't just go referencing musicals at a *Broadway gala*."

His face was so serious, she dissolved into giggles. Daniel's laugh rang out and together, they gazed around the room, enchanted.

Daniel seemed to notice someone across the room. "That's one of the guys from my callback. Should I…"

"Yes, go schmooze. Go." Evie shooed him away.

"You'll be okay?" Max asked her.

"Of course, go have fun."

He squeezed her arm then followed Daniel. For a few more moments, she stood, taking in the room. She then made her way to the bar and ordered drinks for her and Ethan. While she waited, she overheard a conversation close by.

"So you really think he'll show up?"

She kept listening, intrigued by the drama.

"My rep said he would be here. And if he's with her, I'm going to blow up his life. Mr. Keep It Private won't be able to do that for long."

Evie had a feeling she knew who this was. She snuck a glance at the leggy brunette who stood with the posture of a dancer. She was glamorous in a short, sparkly gown.

"I don't blame you," her friend said with a glower.

"Besides, wait until he gets a load of this dress."

Unable to resist, Evie smiled at the woman. "It's a great dress."

"Thank you, that's so sweet," the brunette said. She gave Evie a once-over. "Yours is great, too."

"Thanks." Just then, the bartender approached Evie with her order.

"Here you are, miss. Two seven-and-sevens. With a splash of bitters."

Ethan's signature drink order seemed to get the brunette's attention. She whipped her head towards Evie, her expression venomous. Wincing slightly, Evie wandered away from them, feeling their glares scorching into her bare back.

CHAPTER TWELVE ♫

Alone in the town car, Ethan checked his phone, anxious that Paige would text again. Perhaps it was time he blocked her number. Relieved to see no messages, he tucked it into his jacket then climbed out of the car. The crowd behind the barriers erupted with cheers.

He went down the line, signing Playbills and taking selfies with fans. Fifteen minutes later, breathing a sigh of relief, he stepped into the foyer. Half of the photographers began to shout his name and he walked to the start of the step-and-repeat, posing. Down the line, Dion, one of his old co-stars waved to him as he gave an interview.

Ethan spoke with a few reporters and noticed that Dion was taking a while with the last one on the line. Anxious to see Evie, he rushed through two more chats. Dion was still talking to the last reporter. He was wondering if he could politely skip her when Roger, the blogger who ran OMGCeleb, fought to the front of the line. Groaning inside, Ethan knew he couldn't bypass Roger unless he wanted to read about how rude he was tomorrow. He stepped up to the mic.

"Ethan, so great to see you tonight. What brings you out?"

He gave Roger a grin, aware of the cameras trained on his face. "It's a very important cause, and I'm happy to help out however I can. I haven't seen many of my theatre friends in a while, so I'm looking forward to getting in there."

"Do you have any projects in the works? You know we're dying to see you onstage again."

"Well, I've been doing this live tour, which has been really fun. I'll be starting that up again in a few weeks."

"We are all loving your live shows." Roger's smile grew and he had a dangerous glint in his eye. "One last thing: you know that the internet is blowing up with pictures of you watching a beautiful girl play with your dog. Any comment?"

Ethan wanted to scowl but kept his face neutral. Roger was always the one to try to dig into his personal life, no matter how many times he asked him to respect his privacy. Proving he was a good actor, he gave an easy laugh. "Roger, you know I don't comment on my personal life."

Roger seemed to refrain from rolling his eyes. "Always close to the vest."

Ethan put a hand over his heart. "Always."

Finally breaking away from his duties, Ethan went into the ballroom. As he moved through the cavernous space, he scanned the crowd for Evie's red dress. He couldn't find Max or Daniel, either. Friends and acquaintances stopped him as he searched for her. His patience was waning and he hoped he wasn't being short with anyone. Though he hadn't seen Paige, her presence in the room unnerved him.

He wanted to be with Evie.

At last, he spotted her across the room, talking with Dion. Relief flooded through him at the sight of her face, and he was glad she was with one of his friends. He began to make his way toward her when Paige, in a knockout dress, appeared from out of nowhere. She sauntered over and stopped right in front of him.

"Fancy seeing you here," she purred.

Ethan rolled his eyes and put a chill in his voice. "I'm sure your rep told you I would be."

"There's no need to be bitchy. We can be friends." She stepped closer and kissed him on the cheek.

Closing his eyes and taking a step back, he recognized her manipulation for what it was. He couldn't believe he hadn't seen it when they were dating. She had always been like this, saying one thing and meaning another. Whatever hold Paige had over him, he was certain now that it was long gone. "You called me a coward three hours ago. Why don't you act like an adult and ignore me?"

"Why? So that pretty little thing in the red dress can go home with you?" She pouted.

Seething, Ethan wondered how the hell Paige knew Evie was there with him. "Paige, just leave it. We went our separate ways. I've apologized before, and I'll say it again. I'm sorry I was a dick. But you knew as well as I that this wasn't going to work out. It's been months. Leave it alone."

Paige stepped towards him, eyes narrowed menacingly. "You are an unbelievable asshole, Ethan Carter," she said loudly, causing the people around them to turn and watch.

He gave an exasperated sigh and nodded. "Fine. You can think of me however you want. I know who I am. And I will never think about *you* again. Move on, Paige."

"Move on? Fine. I can move on. But I hope I don't slip up and take a photo tonight. Wouldn't want more photos of her online, would you?"

A rage surged through him. He needed to get away from her and from that whole part of his life. "Don't you fucking dare."

He stalked away, his hands shaking. He needed a drink. He needed Evie.

§

"Yikes, we've all been dreading this," said Dion. He took a sip of his vodka soda and grimaced.

121

Evie had been watching Ethan's exchange with Paige with trepidation. She'd found Dion standing alone at a table and recognized him as one of Ethan's co-stars from *What's Next*. He was kind enough to chat with her as she waited for Ethan to find her, but she didn't give away who she was. She looked at him quizzically.

Dion nodded towards the exchange. "Paige, Ethan Carter's ex. They broke up a few months ago and she loves drama. But...it looks like Ethan's not having it because here he comes. Would you like to meet him?"

She felt a little badly, thinking that she'd perhaps made things worse by talking to Paige earlier. Watching Ethan's expression become increasingly dark troubled her, and she wanted to wrap her arms around him. Unsure how to play this, she simply nodded.

Dion smiled brightly and waved Ethan over. "Ethan, come meet my new friend--"

But Ethan had already gathered Evie in a tight hug. She could feel his heart beating rapidly. "That's much better," he murmured in her ear.

Dion's mouth hung open as he watched this exchange.

Ethan turned to Dion and picked up the drink Evie had gotten him. "Dion, hi. I see you've met my friend Evie."

A look of mock betrayal crossed Dion's face as he looked to Evie.

"I'm sorry. I didn't know what he wanted to say about me so I kept quiet."

Dion chuckled. "Ah yes, our Ethan, so private."

Ethan clinked his glass with Dion's. "What's going on, man, how are you?"

Evie enjoyed listening to the two old friends catch up but could see that Ethan was unsettled. His shoulders were stiff and there was a strain in his voice. She watched him, wondering if there was anything she could do to ease his discomfort.

Ten minutes later, trumpets suddenly sounded and the grand curtain opened, revealing a vast stage and a small orchestra. Evie's hand flew to her heart, and she felt her eyes go wide.

"Are there going to be performances?"

Ethan put his arm around her waist. "Of course. You don't get a bunch of theatre geeks together without expecting that."

For forty-five minutes, Evie was in heaven as she listened to the incredible voices of her favorite Broadway stars. Together, they danced and clapped and sang along, but Ethan still seemed uneasy. When the performers took a break, she turned to him, teary-eyed. "I can't believe I get to be in this room, with all of this talent. And you."

He gazed at her for a long moment. "Come on, I want to show you something." He tugged on her hand and she followed him to a bank of elevators. When the doors opened, he put his hand on the small of her back and led her out onto the dimly lit top balcony, which was deserted. The sound of the party floated up to them, muted. She peeked out onto the floor and gasped.

"Oh, Ethan…"

Below her, the splendor of the room was even more beautiful to behold. It was like watching a movie with all of her favorite characters. She looked for familiar faces and spotted Daniel, in his element, clearly charming someone. Max stood beside him and held his hand. She felt a surge of affection for them both and turned to Ethan. "Look at those two."

She went still. Ethan's jaw was set and he was scowling. His hands gripped the railing so hard his knuckles were white.

"Ethan?"

He closed his eyes and huffed loudly. "I'm sorry. I tried to keep it together."

Evie's stomach clenched. "What do you mean?"

He ran his hands through his hair then clutched the railing again. "Her name was Heather."

Confused, Evie took a step toward him. "Heather?"

"Evie, you don't know why I guard my privacy so strictly." He turned and paced the length of the front row.

"Well, no. I just assumed it's because you want people to see your work, not your personal life."

He stopped and placed his elbows on the railing. He inhaled deeply. "Nine years ago, I was in my first Broadway role. Prince Charming in *Cinderella*. I met Heather at the stage door after a performance, and she was one of many. She was very complimentary and we took a selfie. I didn't have much social media then, just what my agent asked me to have to promote my work. Twitter and Instagram, that was it. That's still it. This was back when I wasn't... you know...me. Before I had a ton of fans and followers.

"She started following me on both platforms. I would interact with her on occasion and she would post that selfie all the time. Like once a week. I thought it was bizarre, but harmless.

"Then she started showing up at the stage door again. So many times, in fact, that security decided to ban her. She messaged me about it and I told her I had nothing to do with it. Every now and again after that, she would send a message, but I started to ignore them.

"Every show I did after that, she would come to the stage door too many times. And every time, security would ban her. By then, I had Julie who was able to help me manage it. Heather would post a ton of Tweets and photos of me, and when they were inappropriate enough, Julie would contact her to take them down.

"And then I started *What's Next.*"

Ethan was pouring his heart out but couldn't seem to look at her. Evie held her breath wondering where this was going.

"That show was a game changer for me. I had done some TV and indie movies by then and I had a pretty good-sized fan base. When that show started running, it positively exploded. I stopped looking at notifications from social media because to be honest, there were a lot. Heather was at the back of my mind, but because I didn't really pay attention, I had no idea how often she was talking about me online.

"And then I started dating someone. I made the mistake of posting a picture of her and me. Heather lost her mind. She harassed me, my girlfriend, anyone she knew that could get in touch with me. She would come to the stage door despite being banned. And she must have followed me home one night because she found out where I lived. I started to see her outside of my apartment. She sent me messages all the time. I would block her, but she would just set up different accounts.

"Then one day, she showed up at my girlfriend's apartment and threatened her. It was terrifying, for her and for me. We didn't know what this woman was capable of. We called the police and both got restraining orders.

"Luckily, that triggered something. She had been convicted for stalking before. We had all the evidence they needed to put her away. And since it wasn't her first offense, she's still in prison. But my girlfriend broke up with me because she thought it might happen again with someone else. And I can't talk about it publicly because it will give her validation, even though it's unlikely she would know.

"That's why my doorman has an NDA. That's why I guard everything so fiercely. If anything happened to anyone I care about just because of my career?"

Suddenly, he turned to her, his eyes stormy. "If anything happened to *you*? I could never forgive myself."

She went to him and embraced him for several long minutes, until she felt his breathing steady. "I'm so sorry, Ethan. That's terrible. What a nightmare."

He gazed at her, a melancholy look on his face. "Thank you. Paige never understood. I can't go public about just anyone."

She raised her eyebrows and glanced down at the floor below them, where the performances were beginning again.

He almost smiled. "I know. It seems like I shouldn't have brought you here. But we haven't let anyone take our picture. And there's no one like her at the moment. Plus, when it's just speculation, it's not so bad. But when a relationship is confirmed...then the crazy really starts."

She laced her fingers through his. "Thank you for trusting me with this."

He drew her hand to his mouth and kissed it. "Thank you for listening."

She wrapped her arms around him again. He stroked his fingers down her back and took a deep breath.

"I have an idea. Let's go downstairs and listen to that gorgeous love song and put this behind us for now."

"Absolutely."

§

Back downstairs, couples paired off to dance during "Some Enchanted Evening." In a quiet corner in the back of the room, despite all that he had just shared with her, Ethan took Evie in his arms. He pressed her hand to his heart and put his other arm around her waist. He felt the strain of the memories leave him, a calm settling in his chest knowing she was so close.

She looked up at him, seeming to search for something, and he lowered his forehead to hers.

"Do you want to get out of here?" he said.

"In a minute." She nuzzled closer and they swayed to the music.

Feeling eyes on him, Ethan lifted his head and looked around. Over Evie's head, he saw Paige, her phone raised in their direction. He glared and pulled Evie closer protectively. She didn't seem to notice a change.

Paige sneered at him, then began typing as she walked away.

CHAPTER THIRTEEN ♫

On the drive back to Brooklyn, Ethan was quiet and pensive. Evie let the silence settle over them and laced her fingers through his.

"If there are photos tomorrow, will you be okay?" he said after a while.

"I think so."

"I'll do whatever I can to protect you."

Evie nestled closer to him. "Thank you. It also helps that I don't live here." She felt him take a shuddering breath.

"I don't want to think about that."

"Me neither."

When they returned to the dark apartment, Ethan immediately took Henry for his walk. Evie was left to herself. She took off her shoes and wandered back to the balcony to enjoy the warm summer air. She was thinking about everything that had happened since Friday, not quite believing it hadn't been months instead of just a few days. She was so lost in thought she didn't hear Ethan come back until he slipped an arm around her waist.

She turned to him. "I'm really going to miss you, Carter."

"I'm really going to miss you, too." He took her by the hand and slowly led her to the bedroom. At the foot of the bed, they stood facing each other. Evie reached up and took his jacket off. She untied his tie deliberately, pulling it off his neck.

He closed his eyes and breathed deeply.

Unbuttoning each button while holding his gaze, Evie slipped his shirt off his shoulders, and then pulled off the crisp white tee underneath it. She paused, gazing at his chest, taking in his marbled form, before she slowly unbuckled his belt and let his pants fall to the floor. She slid his boxer briefs down his body and he stepped out of them.

He stood there, his expression sad and wanting, as she eased the straps of her dress off her shoulders. The red chiffon drifted slowly to the floor as she stepped towards him.

They gazed at each other for a moment before he picked her up and placed her softly on the bed. He lay down next to her.

Ethan propped himself on his elbow and used his free hand to slowly discover her entire body. She breathed deeply as he stroked her breasts, her belly, her thighs. He held her face between his hands as he positioned himself between her legs. He moved in her, deliberately and slowly, holding her gaze throughout. When his release came, he snaked one arm under her, holding her tightly, kissing her.

When he entered her, Evie gasped, her entire body flooded with longing. She wrapped her legs in a knot around him, pulling him deeper, moaning with pleasure. It seemed as if she couldn't get close enough to him. This wasn't like the athletic, passionate sex they'd been having. There was a new intensity to the connection, as if their heartbeats, their very souls, were synchronized. She shuddered and came, her back arching and tears filling her eyes.

Ethan followed a moment later. He held her tightly, feeling on the verge of tears. When he looked down at Evie, he saw a glistening on her cheeks, and let his own tears flow.

They lay, crying sweetly together. After a while he lifted himself free of her, gathered her close, and gently kissed away her tears. The moonlight filtering in through the curtains bathed them in silver.

Ethan stared at the ceiling, thinking. Suddenly he couldn't see any reason to say goodbye to her, not after what just happened. He thought of what Daniel had told him at dinner. "This doesn't...have to be complicated," he said gently.

She kissed his chest.

"Meaning?"

"We could..." he began.

Evie sat up suddenly, her eyes questioning.

"We could do this."

"Ethan..." Evie sounded uncharacteristically uncertain, almost scared.

"Don't you think we could...try?"

She shook her head, as if trying to find the words. "It's not that. It's that the feelings I have for you are so much more than a 'fling', so much more than I thought they would be. And that scares the shit out of me.

"What just happened right here? That was some serious sex. I haven't connected with anyone like that in...not in so long. And I have to go home, I have a whole life back there. Yes, we have an incredible connection but it's just...infatuation. Isn't it? And it's delicious and wonderful, and yes, maybe I can see us together, but that doesn't mean it's going to last, and the risk..."

She was all over the place, as if her logical brain was trying to take over, but her heart wouldn't let it. As if she couldn't find her voice. She looked so small and lost, Ethan's heart broke.

He sat up, facing her, a sharpness in his chest. "I disagree. This is real. And deep. And I know being together would be hard. I just don't see any reason why we have to let it go forever just because we don't live in the same city."

"Ethan," Evie said. A warning.

He got up on his knees and took her face in his hands, desperate now. "No, Evie. No. This is real. I refuse to accept that it isn't."

"Please." She shook her head.

He stared at her, his heart feeling battered. "I want to be with you. After these past three days, I can't imagine anyone else in my life. I can't, Evie. I'm laying it on the line, okay? I could just go ahead and... fall right in love with you. I know myself well enough to know that's true. You are everything--*everything*--I have ever wanted. And I know there's so much I don't know, I do. But I can be this for you, I can be your shelter, I can be your--"

He was babbling. He couldn't help it now that his feelings were out there. It felt like a dam had been broken.

"Ethan, *please.*"

"I don't understand. It doesn't have to be like th--"

"It does. Yes, it *does*. Because I can't lose you."

Ethan froze. What she'd lost, he'd never felt. He didn't know what to do.

Tears began to streak down her cheeks again. "It has to be this way because I've only ever felt like this once in my life. And he fucking *died*. And I can't bear the thought of this going any deeper and then you *leave*--one way or another, you leave. I can't do that again, Ethan. I can't, I can't be that broken again, please..."

She took a deep gasping breath. "I can't, Ethan," she whispered. "I'm not that brave anymore."

Finally, her tears breaking his heart, he could move again. He pulled her close and held her tightly. A tear trickled down his cheek.

"I'm sorry," she whispered, and wiped the moisture from his face.

"You have nothing to be sorry for. I pushed you. I'm the one who's sorry."

She smiled, small and shaky.

"We don't have to say goodbye. Just...see you later," she said. "I want to be in your life."

He kissed her tenderly. "I want that, too."

After a while, Evie said, "I don't want to sleep."

"Me neither."

They talked the rest of the night, dozing intermittently, then waking again to talk and kiss. After taking Henry out at dawn, they had come back and fallen on the bed, their bodies intertwined, finally sleeping deeply.

§

Evie woke up with her head on Ethan's chest, his arms around her. She stretched, waking him. They smiled at each other sleepily.

"We didn't move at all," she said.

"Wow. We really didn't." Ethan sat up and stretched. He caressed her cheek.

"Sorry I cried my face off," she said, a little sheepishly.

"Hey, if we're doing intense, then crying is going to be involved." He kissed her forehead before glancing at the clock. "One o'clock. Four more hours."

Wanting to erase the forlorn look he gave her, she kissed the inside of his wrist and pulled him back down to the bed. Gently, they loved each other. She could feel his heartbeat in sync with her own.

Afterward, Evie texted Daniel that she would meet him at LaGuardia for their flight home. They had decided to put their phones down and ignore everything for a while. They made sandwiches and ate them on the balcony, talking about things that didn't matter, as if trying to stop time and shut out the world.

As they cleaned up the kitchen, Evie noticed his phone lighting up with notifications, one after the other. She elbowed him and nodded at it. He blew out a breath and retrieved it from the bed. Evie followed and sat beside him.

"Photos?" she said.

He nodded and unlocked the phone. "Here we go." He logged into Twitter and was greeted by over three thousand notifications. Paige had tweeted the photo.

Evie leaned over to see. The photo was accompanied with the caption:

@EthanCarter is taken! Sorry, ladies!

Barring the invasion of privacy and trepidation he felt having Evie on the internet, Ethan was almost glad he had the picture. It was he and Evie near the back of the ballroom their hands held against his chest. They were looking at each other like they were the only two people in the universe. He scrolled a bit through his mentions. Some of his followers were devastated, some gave him their best wishes, some were flat out mean. A few were desperate to find out who Evie was. He sighed, locked his phone, and threw it aside. "Welp. That's that."

Evie looked at him expectantly.

"I can't care about upsetting anyone because I have to say goodbye to you in an hour, and that makes me sadder than I can express, so… Whatever."

"You know--"

Before she could finish her sentence, Ethan grabbed her and pulled her to him. He buried his nose in her hair and squeezed her tight. "Go on," he said.

"What you said last night. When you said you could, you know, go right ahead and fall in love with me?"

"I'm a bit much sometimes," he chuckled, "but I meant it."

"Good." She kissed his chest. They gazed into each other's eyes, leaving a thousand things going unsaid.

"I should pack." She got up and wandered around the apartment, picking up her things and throwing them in her suitcase carelessly. She sighed heavily as she zipped her carry on and picked up her shoulder bag. Ethan watched her from his bed, trying not to think of two hours from now, when he would be here without her. She turned to him, finished. It was time to leave.

He put on his Chucks, and then took her hand. "Evelyn O'Hara, this has been the best four days I've spent in a long, long time."

"Buddy, you have no idea."

He kissed her lingeringly, unwilling to let her go. Her phone sounded and she reluctantly pulled away.

"That's my leave-for-the-airport reminder."

He gazed down into her green eyes, trying to imprint the sight on his memory forever.

"I guess we better go." He picked up her suitcase and she her shoulder bag. On their way out the door, she knelt down and tousled Henry's head. "'Bye, sweet pup." They headed to the garage where he put her suitcase in the trunk as she settled in the passenger seat.

He got in, staring straight ahead. "If my car doesn't start, it's a sign," he said, only half joking. But the engine turned over, and he groaned. "Stupid German engineering."

Evie picked up the AUX cable and plugged in her phone, scrolling to "Skinny Love." Bon Iver's melancholy song serenaded them as Ethan drove.

Forty minutes later, he pulled into the cell phone lot at LaGuardia. Once he'd pulled her suitcase from the trunk and set it down, they looked at each other for several moments. Finally, Evie stepped into his arms, her action mirroring the first hug they'd shared, full of warmth.

"I can't stand this," he said, his voice cracking.

Evie hugged him tighter, and he felt her take a deep breath to keep from crying.

"This isn't goodbye forever." She gazed at his beautiful face, memorizing every part of it. "This is just 'see you later'. We can talk, and I'll be back, and maybe you could come to Chicago."

He stroked a finger along her jawline. "Absolutely. Don't say goodbye. Please."

She checked her watch. "I better go."

They kissed deeply, with his hands on her waist and the back of her neck, hers tangling in his hair.

"Text me when you land, okay?" he said, reluctant to let her go.

She nodded. "Until next time, Carter."

"Next time, Freckles."

She walked away, bags in hand, and then, just before disappearing into the terminal, looked back and waved. He waved back, turned, and got back in the car.

§

Evie went through security without incident. She walked to her gate and sat down, fighting tears. When Daniel appeared he immediately came to put his arms around her.

"Oh, sweet baby, are you okay?"

"Not right now. But I will be," she assured him. He kissed the top of her head.

Evie took the window seat. For the entire four-and-a-half-hour flight, she tried to read and failed, so she settled on going over every single perfect moment from the past four days. It comforted her. When they landed, she switched her phone off airplane mode and a dozen photos from Ethan came through. She scrolled through, her heart aching, and texted him back.

> Safe on the ground. Can't believe I'm not there with you.

> Henry is wandering around looking for you. I'm certain he misses you. Not as much as I do, though.

Daniel offered to go home with her, but she just wanted to be alone. When she entered her apartment, she was greeted by the desperate meow of her cat. She gathered him in her arms, sat down on the floor and cried until she didn't have anything left.

§

Ethan stared straight ahead for a few moments, wanting to run after Evie. He pounded the steering wheel twice with his fist, before picking up his phone and dialing Julie.

"Ethan, I assume you saw the photo. You have a girlfriend, according to Twitter," Julie said, when she answered.

"I don't, but I figured I owed you a call."

"Paige. I can't believe she posted that picture."

"I know."

"But there's nothing I can do, really, you *were* with Evie in public," Julie reminded him gently.

"It's fine, Jules," he snarled. He rubbed the bridge of his nose. He'd never been short with Julie before.

"Are you okay?"

"She just got on the plane."

"Anything I can do?"

Ethan felt his throat tighten. He clenched his jaw.

"Ethan?"

"Sorry, Jules. No. I'm okay. Thanks." He said goodbye and hung up. Once inside his apartment, he stood for a moment, feeling the stillness. Evie's fun, sweet presence was gone.

He sent her their photos so she would have them when she landed, and then threw himself on his bed. Henry jumped up beside him and nudged his head under Ethan's arm. He fell into a fitful sleep.

It was nearly ten when he woke up, disoriented. He checked his phone. She had just landed. He texted her back and took Henry out. Afterward he went back to bed, where he stayed the next day until noon.

He was right. When he woke up, everything was gray.

CHAPTER FOURTEEN ♫

Evie stood in the hallway, her hand on the doorknob of Liam's den. A shudder went through her as she pushed open the door. She took a gasping breath and glanced around the room. A layer of dust covered the TV stand and bookshelves. The pillows on the sofa were still indented where he'd sat. She buried her face in one of his discarded hoodies, thinking she could still smell a trace of him. As she boxed up his books and guitars, her tears came freely. She let them.

It had been two weeks since she'd left Ethan behind. She felt forever changed. Again. They spoke every day, something that Evie had not expected and now did not want to live without. But being surrounded by memories of Liam was disorienting, and she finally felt it was time. She moved through the condo and removed photos and mementos.

After taking everything to either her storage unit or the shelter at which she volunteered, she stood in the dining room contemplating the one photo she had kept on display.

She kissed two fingers and gently placed them on Liam's heart.

Thank you.

A peace settled in her heart. She felt cleansed.

Curiosity got the better of her a few days later. She searched social media for the photo Paige posted, and found dozens of posts about herself. Ethan's fans speculated about who she was and what was going on with the two of them. But as time passed and nothing new about her was posted, the fervor died down. Ethan assured her that he and Julie were monitoring for any alarming activity, but so far, it was all normal Ethan Carter obsession.

Two weeks after her trip down the rabbit hole of Ethan fans, Evie lay on her bed, staring at the ceiling, having just finished her daily chat with him. What was she doing, giving him so much space in her heart? She wasn't going to move to New York. How could she, when her whole life was here?

Wasn't it?

She was twirling her phone in her hands when it rang.

"Hello, my love."

"Evie," Daniel all but shrieked, "I have another callback. Let's get back to New York."

§

Six weeks after their first fortuitous visit, Evie and Daniel landed in New York again. The September air promised autumn. When they got to the cab line, Evie told him to break a leg and got into the next cab. She gave the driver Ethan's now familiar address. Had that incredible weekend been real, or had they imagined their feelings since? Her stomach seemed full of butterflies that intensified as the cab pulled onto Ethan's block.

The doorman buzzed her in. "Well hello, young lady. Great to see you again."

"You have no idea." Evie beamed at him as she called the elevator. It was the longest ride of her life. When the doors finally slid open, she practically ran down the hall to Ethan's door.

She walked in, expecting to be tackled by Henry. Instead she was greeted by candlelight, John Legend's voice, wildflowers, and Ethan.

Steady, strong Ethan.

His smile shone at her. She dropped her bag and went to him slowly, her eyes dancing. She took his hands and molded her body to his. He embraced her and kissed her, long and slow. Her anxiety melted away, replaced by the feeling that all was right in her world.

"Evie." He cradled her face gently in his hands. "I have never wanted anything more than this moment, right here."

She couldn't find the words to convey her feelings, so she rose onto her tiptoes and kissed him. He led her to the bedroom where he undressed her as if he were unwrapping a present. Eagerly, she tugged his clothes off of him and they fell onto the bed together. Ethan propped himself up on one elbow and gazed at her body. She hardly dared to breathe. A heady feeling rose in her as he stared at her and she felt a flush creep up her chest. When he finally reached out and stroked her belly, she shivered in anticipation. He gave her a soft smile.

"I didn't think I would get to see you again. Not like this." He seemed to relish every moment being next to her.

She curled herself into him, winding her hands in his hair. "This is heaven."

Every touch, every kiss, she cherished. She felt their connection reinforce, the tether between them grow stronger.

Afterward, he held her in his arms, his eyes closed, his lips turned up slightly.

"I'm so glad I came back."

He drew her closer. "I never want you to leave again." He kissed the top of her head.

She stilled and felt her heart skip a beat. *Never?*

The next few days were bliss. Ethan couldn't get enough of Evie. It wasn't just the physical connection he felt, but the ease with which she reached for his hand, the way they laughed together. He knew what she was feeling must be complicated, but from what he'd learned from his married friends, this is how it was supposed to be. Effortless.

Walking around Greenwich Village after dinner one evening, she looked up at him, her green eyes inquisitive.

"What is it?"

"This just feels--" She seemed to falter, trying to find the right word.

He put his arm around her and drew her close. "I've never been with someone who felt so right."

She kissed him then, with a feeling behind it that he couldn't comprehend.

The third day, Evie accompanied Ethan to a rehearsal for his next show in Boston. As she watched and listened, she marveled at his incredible talent once again. He was energetic and goofy, playing to Evie, laughing his way through his set.

That night, during dinner in his apartment, he told her that his reps had finally confirmed a show at the House of Blues in Chicago for mid-November.

"I can't wait. You are going to love Chicago so much. I'm going to show you around and I want tickets for your show, and oh my god, Carter. We are going to have so much fun." She threw herself into his lap and kissed him enthusiastically.

He laughed through her kisses. "You know I've been to Chicago before."

"Shut up and let me have this," she said.

Ethan knew now more than ever that he and Evie should be together. Remembering their last night of that first weekend, though, stopped him from saying anything more about it. He decided to let her be the one to bring up their future.

He didn't have to wait long. As they were saying goodbye at the airport again, both of them far happier than they were the last time, she looked him straight in the eye with that steely gaze that meant she was about to be blunt.

"This isn't over, Carter. I will see you in a few weeks," she said.

"I'm so glad to hear you say that."

"I'm not making any promises, but clearly this thing between us...it's supposed to be happening."

"I fully agree," he said. He wrapped her in a bear hug, breathed in her scent and kissed her again.

She had a twinkle in her eyes when she looked up at him. "Until next time, Carter."

"Next time, Freckles." He tweaked her nose, and then watched her walk away.

He put his hand over his heart, feeling so much for her that he felt he could move mountains.

She turned around, gave him that sweet smile, and waved one more time.

His heart swelled, and then he knew. This was what everyone talked about. It wasn't the puppy love he'd felt for his first girlfriend, or the desperation he'd felt with Paige. This feeling was deeper, steadier, and unquestioning.

He was falling in real, true love.

As Evie walked away from Ethan, her heart was ridiculously full. She was wildly uncertain of the future, but knew that whatever it might hold, they'd be doing it together.

She met Daniel at the gate just as she had weeks before. This time he was beaming.

"How did it go? Sorry I haven't checked in. I've been--ahem--busy."

He grinned at her. "Bet you were. And I had Max, so I guess we're even."

"So? How was the callback?"

"Okay. Listen. You know how you and I say the things out loud to each other that we would never *ever* say to anyone else?"

"Yes. Go."

"I think--" He took a deep breath. "I'm gonna be on Broadway."

Evie gaped at him for several long seconds then emitted a squeal and threw her arms around him. He laughed aloud and hugged her back. On the plane ride home, as they drank champagne and planned Daniel's future surrounding his Broadway fame, Evie's spirits were lighter than they had been for a long, long time.

When they landed, tipsy and still giddy, Evie turned her phone back on. Ethan had texted, asking her to call. That was odd. She did, as they waited to get off the plane.

"Miss me already?" she said, when he answered.

"I do but listen. Someone found us in the Village the other night. There are photos."

Evie was only a little concerned. "Is this different than the gala photos? Is anyone being creepy?"

"Well, no, not like...not like Heather. But..."

"Ethan."

His words came out in a rush. "Somehow, someone must have found out your name."

After arguing with him over the dinner bill, Ethan had finally let her pay. Her name would have been on the credit card slip.

She wasn't ready for this. She took a deep breath.

"So? They'll find my Twitter and Instagram, but I have them on lockdown. Everything is private. There's nothing for them to find."

Ethan sighed. "There is though, love. I wanted to warn you before you saw it. They found everything...about Liam. It's blowing up."

Evie began to tremble.

"I'm so sorry Evie, Julie is on it. She's trying to curb it, but I wanted you to know. If it comes to it, I'm going to Tweet something. Just don't look, okay? Until we can get it under control?"

She took another deep breath. "I'm still on the plane. I have to process this. I'll call you later."

"Okay. I understand. And Evie? I'm so sorry."

141

She could hear the concern in his voice. "It's not your fault. I'll call you later."

Daniel had clearly gleaned what happened. He held Evie's hand on the way home and didn't say a word. He'd always understood when she needed silence.

They got out of the cab in front of her building. He said, "Do you want me to come up?"

She thought about it, then shook her head. "No. I need to… I need to just confront it head on. And have whatever feelings I'm going to have. I'll see you tomorrow?"

Daniel hugged her, and he went off to walk the block and a half to his home.

Evie dropped her purse and carry-on inside the door, fed Norman, and sat down in front of her laptop. She took a deep breath and navigated to Tumblr. A couple of blogs had posted a photo of her and Ethan in the Village, giving her name. There were also a couple of bloggers who derided those, pleading to keep their crush's privacy. Others did not believe they owed it to him.

> Our dork's girlfriend is named Evelyn O'Hara! I did a search and get this. She had a husband who died. She lives in Chicago, and does a bunch of volunteer work, but how pathetic does she have to be to go after someone barely a year after her husband kicks it? Gross.

> I think you're being harsh, wouldn't you go after Ethan's stupid face if your husband was dead?

> He's barely been dead a year. She's disgusting.

> I feel really bad for her. But still. That seems really weird.

> If my husband died, I wouldn't be able to breathe, let alone start fucking a Broadway star.

Evie hadn't noticed that she was crying. She rubbed her hands over her face and continued to scroll. After punishing herself enough with Tumblr, she opened the Twitter app on her phone. She wandered the condo as she deleted messages and follow requests. She was surprised to find that a lot of fans wished her well. But there were many that didn't.

She turned off the capability to get direct messages and deleted all her follower requests. She did the same on Instagram, where there was more of the same.

She Googled her own name, wanting to know what would be found by those that did. Dozens of articles popped up about the accident, Liam's memorial and obituary and further down, her old work information and the list of organizations where she volunteered.

The thought of these monsters learning about Liam, knowing his name--her *husband*, her private pain--became too much. A sob escaped her and she curled herself into a ball on her bed. Emotionally exhausted, she ignored Ethan's concerned texts and tried to sleep.

The clock glowed 2:47 a.m. when Evie woke from a fitful sleep. She threw an arm over her eyes. She could tell how puffy they were. Tossing about for the next few minutes, she conceded that sleep would not come. She stared at the ceiling, the rumble of Norman's purring next to her a small comfort. Another ten minutes went by, and she knew there was only one way to make her feel okay again.

"Evie. God. I've been worried."

At the sound of Ethan's voice, she felt a little calmer. "What the hell is wrong with people?"

"I don't know, love. I don't know. I'm so sorry. I feel so badly. Julie's done some damage control, but that shitty

143

blog OMGCeleb is writing an article or something tomorrow. She said there's nothing she can do to stop it. I'm so sorry. Should I come to Chicago?"

Evie rubbed her face. "No, no of course not. You have a show in three days."

"I don't... I don't know what to say. I understand if you want to just...quit." His voice caught.

She sat up quickly. "Not an option, Carter," she said, making her tone forceful and self-confident.

He sighed audibly before saying, "I'm going to say something."

"You don't have to."

"I want to, truly. I need to. Hearing your voice like this..."

"Well, then do what you need to. But maybe this is a blessing in disguise. Now they know. There's nothing they can dig up anymore. Might as well go all in. You're clearly seeing someone. They can deal with it."

After a long silence, Ethan said, "I guess that makes sense. Try and get some more sleep. I'll call you tomorrow."

"Okay. And Carter..."

"Yeah, Freckles?"

"This sucks, but as long as you're mine, I don't regret our time together for a second."

"Neither do I."

Evie woke in the morning to a new follower on Instagram and Twitter, and a text that said:

> All in, right? I know the fans always check to see who I'm following. Figured I might as well since it's out there.

She smiled, approved Ethan, and deleted everyone else's requests. Curious, she scrolled through her Twitter feed. He had Tweeted an hour ago.

@EthanCarter: Be kind to one another. I love you all & your support means the world, but please respect my privacy. Thank you.

This was followed by messages of support and love from his fans. Evie felt better, partly because the shock of seeing the articles about Liam's death was wearing off. As she was scrolling through the messages, Ethan texted again.

Sending you this because it's getting around. Don't want you to stumble on it.

A link followed and she clicked on it. OMGCeleb had indeed written an "article," accompanied by an old press photo of Ethan and photos of them in the Village, at the gala, and in the park with Henry.

CARTER'S TRAGIC LOVER

Big news in the Broadway community! Broadway star and super hunk, Ethan Carter (you know him from everything, don't make me list them) has taken a lovaaah!

That's right kittens, we're devastated, too. But we're not as devastated as his new lady was a little over a year ago, when her husband straight up died. We're not even kidding. Not only is she a gorgeous redhead, but she has a tragic backstory to go with all that hair. A sensitive hunk like Ethan could hardly resist. And this must be the girl he was singing to at his show a while back, right?

She's also apparently jobless, but volunteers all over Chicago, where she lives. Maybe she's rich herself, but we hope for Ethan's sake she isn't a gold digger.

Truly found love in a hopeless place! Mazel tov, babies!

(Carter's rep had no comment.)

Evie closed the browser and texted Ethan back:

I feel gross. He's gross. But I do feel better this morning.

He replied:

I'm so glad. I'll call you later, heading out to meetings/rehearsal. XO

§

Ethan headed to Julie's office, who had done what she could to deal with the social media explosion. He collapsed in the guest chair in her office. She regarded him from across her desk, as if she didn't know where to begin.

Julie sighed. "Well, it's out there."

"Yep."

"How are you feeling?"

He sat forward, rested his forearms on his thighs, and gave her question some thought. "You know, the only thing that pisses me off is that Evie's hurt. As far as us being out in the open, I don't really care. I wish our relationship were more defined--or defined at all. And I'm not going to specifically say anything about Evie. As long as you have any potential Heathers under control, for the first time, I don't mind the world knowing my business."

"Okay. I've dealt with what I could, and what you said this morning seems to have made a lot of them feel bad."

He drummed his fingers on the arms of the chair, feeling his shoulders grow tense. "Julie, there isn't anyone to be concerned about, is there?"

She gave him an understanding smile. "No, definitely not."

"Okay." He relaxed. "If you're sure. Good. That's good."

"I'm sure. One hundred percent." Julie picked up a pen and twirled it through her fingers.

"Now, off the professional track here, are you…in love with her? Like, what's happening here? Because at first it was just a fling, and you haven't spent all that much time together, but I have honestly never seen you like this."

Ethan sat back and grinned. "No comment."

Julie laughed. "I've trained you well."

§

The next time she felt brave, Evie checked social media again. She found many posts referencing Ethan's Tweet. The reprimand had worked.

Oh no, we pissed off him off.

He's mad at us guys, we need to stop.

I feel pretty horrible. Wish them well. Still really devastated though.

She sighed deeply, feeling a profound gratitude to Ethan. She knew it took a lot for him to say something publicly. Since it seemed the fans were going to stop speculating, she decided to move on as well. What else could she do? Decision made, she Facetimed Ethan. When he answered, she felt all the tension of the past few days waning and began to laugh. She couldn't seem to control it.

He arched an eyebrow. "What's so funny?"

"You're just so fucking good looking, it's ridiculous," she said through her laughter.

He seemed to share her joy. "What are you feeling, Freckles?" he said, when their laughter tapered off.

"Besides my heart about to burst at the sight of your face? Actually? I feel okay. The fuss seems to have died down. Your fans don't like it when you're disappointed in them."

"And about them knowing your name? And everything? You're okay?" He peered at her through the screen, as if trying to get a read on her.

She shrugged. "What they found is…a part of me. And it happened, so I just need to accept that and move on. You know?"

"You're something else." He shook his head. "I have some good news for a change. I got my tickets for Chicago. I'm coming in two days before the show and staying for two after. I did not, however, book a hotel."

"Because you're staying with me," she said without hesitation.

He beamed. "Damn right."

"And I get you all to myself for four whole days?"

"All five actually, a few interviews and the concert aside, I'm all yours."

"Damn right," she echoed.

CHAPTER FIFTEEN ♫

Ethan stepped out into the chilly Chicago air and scanned O'Hare's busy arrival area, looking for Evie.

"Hey, handsome." He looked to his left and saw her in a silver SUV. When she got out to open the trunk, he picked her up and kissed her, and then put his suitcase in the back.

"You're a sexy driver," he told her as she navigated the hectic Chicago traffic.

"I have a feeling you think I'm a sexy most-things." At the first stop light, she turned to him. "So, my house. Are you going to have any feelings about it?"

"Because you lived in it with Liam?"

"Yeah."

"I have no idea," he answered honestly.

Her duplex was flooded with natural light and filled with eclectic but tasteful furniture. The art was chosen carefully, an assorted array of vintage prints and modern paintings that somehow gelled together and made the space all Evie's own. In the dining room, in a gold frame on the sideboard, he noticed a photo of her and Liam on their wedding day.

Gently, he picked it up and studied the photo. It was winter on Lake Michigan. Evie was wearing a gold and ivory gown, Liam, a black tuxedo jacket. They were smiling joyously at each other. Two thoughts ran through his mind. The first, that he was, surprisingly, a little jealous. But more important, that he'd seen that look on her face directed right at him. A familiar thrill shivered down his spine. He turned to look at her. She wasn't meeting his eyes.

"I... I couldn't take all of them down," she said.

He set the photo back in place and took a step toward her. Taking one of her hands, he tipped her face up to his. "Thank you for letting me see that. You made an absolutely beautiful bride."

She squeezed his hand. "Thank you."

He caressed her cheek and tenderly kissed her. "I love your place."

"Thank you...my lord." She curtseyed.

The heaviness of the last few moments eased and he chuckled at their inside joke. "My lady, I confess to be starving. And I'd love a shower. Plane grime." He picked at his sweater and wrinkled his nose.

Pressing her nose into his chest, she inhaled deeply. "Nope. You smell perfect. Shall we order some food?"

Ethan was freshly showered when their bahn mi was delivered. They were nearly finished with their meal when Norman appeared to beg for his dinner.

Evie gestured to the cat and rose to get his food. "If you want to feed him, he'll love you forever."

"If you say so." Ethan opened the can of food and Norman curled around his legs, meowing, as he scooped it into his dish. Once the dish was on the floor, Norman ate greedily and purred loudly. Ethan stroked him.

"How about that? We're friends now."

Evie felt a jolt in her heart and she tugged on his hand. "Ethan."

He turned from the cat, a smile still on his face. As he gazed at her, his smile faded. The deep blue of his eyes reflected her need. "Hey, you."

"Hey." She pulled him towards the bedroom, her heart pounding. Letting go of his hand, she lit a candle. Behind her, he put his hands on her waist and tenderly kissed her neck. She snaked an arm behind her and wound her fingers in his hair. An intense urgency overcame her, a want so deep it was frightening. She turned and stripped off his clothes, and then pushed him onto the bed.

Looking into his eyes, she undressed before him, watching his breathing grow heavy. Wanting to feel every part of him, she slid on top of him. Every part of her skin called for his touch.

His hand cradled her face and she paused to gaze at his perfect lips. She savored every moment when her lips met his. Somehow, she knew he could feel this passion, this urgency. As her hands ran up his chest, she felt him shiver.

Taking her by the waist, he positioned her on top of him and gasped when she brought him deep inside of her. With what seemed to be a desperation, he wrapped his arms around her and pulled her closer. Ethan filled her every sense. She was helpless for want of him. She bit his bottom lip and cried out when she climaxed.

His grip had not loosened some long, delicious moments later. Her breathing began to slow, but she could still feel the flush of her chest. She drew back and looked into his eyes.

"Evie...wow..." He wound his fingers in her hair.

"I needed you."

"I needed you, too."

That night, she slept soundly and didn't wake up until the sun peeked through the curtains.

§

In the morning, Ethan woke before Evie. He kissed her shoulder and she burrowed further into her pillow. Smiling softly, he got ready for the day and made them breakfast. He felt as at home in her place as she did in his.

"Ooh omelets." Evie breezed by him and sat down at the kitchen table. The sweet smell of lavender wafted over him. He brought her a plate and kissed her good morning. "What's on the agenda today?"

Ethan brought up the calendar on his phone. "Let's see. Interview, another interview, then I'm free for the evening."

"Do you need a ride to these interviews?"

"As a matter of fact, I do."

"Allow me to be your chauffer." She took a bite of her omelet. "Anything you want to do tonight?"

"Since I have a show tomorrow, I just want to relax." He reached across the table and ran his thumb over her hand. "With you."

She entwined her fingers with his.

As he gave his interviews to the Chicago news station and the Chicago Reader, he could see Evie out of the corner of his eye. It was almost strange to have her witness this performative side of himself after all the private moments they'd shared.

Weird but not weird.

Why hadn't any of this ever felt weird? For as fast as his heart opened for her, for as strange as it was to be thousands of miles apart most of the time, nothing about this relationship felt wrong.

Cuddled up in her bed that night, Evie put on a mindless home renovation show. Something must have exhausted her, because she fell asleep quite early, still in his arms. He watched her face as she slept, feeling peaceful. After a while, he pulled his arm out from under her and laid her on the pillow. He kissed her softly, turned off the bedside lamp, and fell asleep himself.

§

Ethan's eyes snapped open. The bedside clock read 6:43a.m.

Show day.

He was not getting back to sleep. He lay still for a while and laid out his set list in his mind. He wondered if he should switch the place of two of the songs. They hadn't felt right in the last couple of performances. His mind raced and he began to stress. Next to him, Evie stirred.

He rolled over and propped himself up on one elbow. He smiled softly as he caressed her bare back, feeling the stress wash away. He'd ask her when she woke up. She was practically magic--she would know. He scooted closer to her, snaked an arm under her, and kissed her shoulder.

"Good morning," she murmured.

Burying his face in her neck, his other hand explored the rest of her body. "Good morning." He nipped at her neck and she gasped. "You make everything better, did you know that?"

"I'm beginning to...Ethan..." She arched her back against him. "I feel like I'm dreaming."

"Me too." He kissed her with a hunger he was sure would never be sated.

Some long delicious moments later, she gasped for breath. She was trembling.

"That was a hell of a way to wake up, Carter."

He squeezed her closer. "Question. Should 'I'd Rather Be Sailing' come before or after 'Moving Too Fast'?"

"Before. It's a little sad, and 'Moving Too Fast' is so cute and funny. It'll cheer everyone up."

He sighed into her neck. "I knew you'd know."

She sat up and stretched and turned to him. He searched her eyes.

It was that moment, that still moment of perfect tension, right before the hero of the story says *I love you* for the first time. Ethan put a palm to her cheek and had opened his mouth to say it. But before he could, Evie kissed him and headed to the bathroom.

Dropping his hand, he flopped down onto the pillow. He thought about the consequences of telling her, what scrutiny she'd endure that she hadn't already. He thought about the photo in the dining room, how he hadn't wanted to push Evie. But he knew he wasn't wrong about his feelings. He knew this was real.

He heard the shower start and rolled over. The cat was staring at him from the bench at the foot of the bed. "What?"

Norman continued to stare.

"I think I love your mom," Ethan told him.

Norman yawned.

"You...are not a dog." He rolled his eyes and began to gather his necessities for his show.

Expectations of his performance were running through his head. He wondered if his dumb heart would talk about Evie before his brain could stop it and guessed it would.

Once they were both showered and dressed, Evie practically skipped to her favorite neighborhood brunch spot. He watched the sunlight play in her hair. "You're pretty chipper this morning."

She turned to look at him. A wide grin spread across her face. "I really like having you here."

Evie sipped her coffee once their meals were ordered. "So how does today work?"

"I have to be down at the House of Blues for soundcheck at three. Then I'll chill backstage, get some dinner with the crew. Meet-and-greet line begins at six. The question and answer section starts at seven. And I'll be onstage by eight. I have your VIP tickets. You'll be in the center balcony. I didn't want you to have to fight for a spot on the floor."

"Excellent. I almost got crushed at a Killers concert once. Glad that won't happen again. It's so cool that you're playing House of Blues. I wonder if they've ever had a straight-up showtunes concert before."

"Lucky they had an opening. Lucky that I got to come here."

She squeezed his hand and sighed happily. "Very."

When their meals came, she said, "Should we show up for the Q&A?"

He thought about it, chewing a piece of bacon. "That's up to you. There were only thirty tickets for it, so it's a relatively small crowd. And they'll definitely know who you are. These are my--how do I say this--most *devoted* fans."

Evie nodded. "I'll think about it." She spread strawberry jam on her toast. "Hey, Danny said New York was supposed to call by today. We'll finally know if he's Broadway bound."

Ethan felt a twinge of excitement. "That would be amazing. But I've never gotten a call on time. Hope his hopes aren't too high."

She caught his eye and looked at him for a long, loaded moment. Was she thinking about what would change if Daniel moved to New York?

"I'm sure he's a ball of nerves. But I also know he feels good about the work he put in. My fingers are crossed."

"Mine, too."

Once back at Evie's place, he double checked that his bag for the concert was ready and then found he couldn't settle to anything. She watched him pace from a window to the couch and back again.

"Hey, buddy, what do you need?"

He paused, not wanting to offend her. "Honestly? I think I need to go for a run and be by myself before I go downtown. Is that okay?"

She stood and kissed his cheek. "Go get 'em, tiger."

He felt like he could run forever on the fuel of that one little phrase.

§

"I think he almost said he loves me."

Daniel stopped short, a roll in one hand, his butter knife in the air. His eyebrows shot up. "Did he now?"

"This morning. After morning sex. There was a look in his eyes."

"There's always a look in their eyes after morning sex."

"Ha, ha. You know what I mean."

Over the din of their fellow diners, Frank Sinatra serenaded them. The steakhouse was old Chicago, all dim lighting, tin ceiling, and fancy tablecloths. Evie half expected to see Al Capone walk through the doors. Daniel finished buttering his bread.

"So does he love you?"

She looked at the dancing flames in the fireplace near their table. "I don't know."

"Maybe a more important question is, do you love him?" He gave her a probing look.

She took a gulp of wine. "I don't know."

"Well, glad that's settled."

She chuckled. "It's strange. I feel like in New York, it's this big fantasy. Gorgeous Broadway star, glittering parties, singing duets. But here--here at home--Ethan feels real. Our connection or relationship or whatever this is. It all feels true. When he was so far away, I could, I don't know, not think about the reality of where this might go. But now? Now I feel like I have to make some sort of decision."

"Did he ask you to?"

Evie shook her head. "I don't think he would. But without any definition, how can this go on?"

"You don't have to decide anything you don't want to. Not until you're ready."

She blew him a kiss and watched him glance nervously at his phone. "They'll call."

"It's Saturday night. They probably won't."

"Ethan said he'd never gotten a call on time."

"I guess that makes me feel better." He groaned. "This is torture."

She laid a hand on his arm. "They'll call."

Grasping her hand, Daniel took a shaky breath. "They'll call."

"Okay folks, Ethan is going to come out in just a second, and he's happy to answer your questions. A few guidelines: not a lot is off limits, but please refrain from anything too personal or inappropriate. We invite questions about his career and his hobbies," Max said to the audience of about thirty fans standing in front of him. A shiver of anticipation ran through the crowd. When Ethan appeared onstage in a hoodie, carrying a water bottle, they cheered.

Smiling genially, he sat down on the lip of the stage as Max chose audience members to ask questions.

"My favorite role…that's a great question. I've played so many different parts, but I think my favorite had to be Curly in my high school's production of *Oklahoma*." The audience tittered. He snickered too. "I know it seems silly, but I was only a sophomore and I got the lead. That was a big deal. That's when I really fell in love with performing and knew it could be a career. It really set me on the path to this stage. I didn't play baseball that summer, I went to theatre camp. And from then on, that was it. And hey, I made one of my best friends." He gestured to Max, who smiled widely and pointed to the next questioner.

"How's Henry?" she asked.

"Oh man, he's hilarious. He does this thing now when he stretches: he lets out this huge 'AWOOO'." Ethan imitated Henry's howl and the audience burst out laughing. "I swear he only does it to be dramatic."

"What's your favorite song to sing in the shower?"

"Ooh, another good one. Depends on my mood. If I'm feeling melancholy, I'll go with Ed Sheeran's sadder songs. When I'm angry, I'll scream along with Rage Against the Machine. And if I'm feeling triumphant? *Dreamgirls*, all of Effie's songs."

The audience guffawed, no doubt imagining him belting out "Love You I Do." After a few more questions, Ethan stood.

"Thank you all so much. I will see you in about half an hour." He waved and headed offstage. Just before he disappeared beyond the curtains, he looked up to the balcony where Evie was standing. How had he known she was there?

§

Ethan must have told the staff her name because they were escorted up to the ornate balcony immediately upon arrival. From there, they could see the whole stage and the empty floor in front of it, soon to be filled with more enthusiastic fans. The high ceiling made for perfect acoustics.

"The star treatment," Daniel said. He bought them drinks from the upstairs bar. As Ethan answered questions, Evie sipped her vodka soda and felt her heart fluttering in her chest. She knew he was funny, but it was thrilling to hear others laugh at his stories. He seemed so at ease with his fans. Despite his troubles in the past, he seemed to genuinely enjoy getting to enhance their experience. He glanced up at the balcony just before he left the stage and beamed right at her.

Excitement flooded her when the house doors opened. As the space around them filled up with Ethan's fans, she heard snippets of eager chatter.

"Do you think he'll do 'Corner of the Sky'?"

"Did you hear he's probably going to be Wesley in *The Princess Bride*?"

"I watched the live TV *Company* again last night. I cry when he cries."

Evie bit her lower lip in anticipation and grabbed Daniel's hand. He joined her when she hopped up and down. The energy in the room ramped up when the lighting changed five minutes before curtain.

Beside her, Daniel started and pulled his phone out of his pocket. He paled. "My agent."

Evie gasped. "Oh my god, go, go!" She chewed her lip as she watched him push his way through the dense crowd. Time seemed to slow almost to a stop as she waited for both his return and for Ethan's show to begin. She wasn't sure which had her more breathless.

When Daniel returned, he was stone faced. "Nothing yet," he said. "They were confirming a few schedule things."

Evie groaned. "Mean!"

Daniel chuckled, just as the lights went down. Ethan's band and backup singers walked onstage and an enthusiastic cheer rose up from the crowd. The lights faded to black and a tremor went through the room.

Ethan's silky voice filled the room with the beginning verse of "Take A Chance On Me" from *Mamma Mia*. The audience erupted with screams so loud, Evie felt the roof was going to fall in. The lights came up on him, in complete command of the stage. She leaned over the railing, marveling at his charm as he told stories and talked to the audience between songs.

She shivered her way through his rendition of "Corner of the Sky". "Not While I'm Around" got her teary eyed. It wasn't just the trained voice and the innate talent that Ethan possessed. It was the way he invited the audience in to share his journey through the stories of the songs. He opened himself up to the whole room, letting them feel everything he felt.

That she got to know him, to talk to him, to be with him, was a gift.

"He is incredible," Daniel said in her ear during "I'd Rather Be Sailing."

She nodded.

When the song finished, he started "Moving Too Fast." She smiled smugly. She was right--it was a perfect transition.

Toward the end of the concert, he brought a stool to center stage. "How many of you have ever been in love?"

he asked. She saw him chuckle at the shouts of "I love you, Ethan." from several corners of the hall.

"I love you, too." He settled onto the stool. "I'm not talking about that blistering, desperate love, the kind that keeps your stomach in knots, that makes you believe if you don't talk to each other for twenty-four hours, that means it's over. I'm talking about that real, slow, steady love. The kind that doesn't freak you out, that doesn't make you want to rush it because you know it's real. And you want to say it--you're desperate to say it--but you don't know how."

Evie took short, shallow breaths. What was happening?

He seemed to hesitate. "Anyway, here's one of my favorite showtunes about love."

His pianist played a lilting intro and he began to sing "If I Loved You" from *Carousel.*

As the last note faded, the audience erupted with cheers and applause. The whole room was thick with emotion. Evie was surprised to find tears rolling down her cheeks. Wrapped up in the love song, she had almost forgotten they were in a room with hundreds of other people. Ethan seemed to sing directly to her.

Which he was. Wasn't he?

Was he?

Oh my.

Ethan smiled one more time up at the balcony. She laid her hand over her heart, just as Ethan did the same.

"Thank you," he said, before turning to his band. His last few songs went by in a blur and he said goodnight. The continued cheering brought him back onstage and he performed a medley of songs from musical theatre's most notorious villains as an encore.

When the house lights went up, Evie still stood, hands braced on the railing in front of her with her heart hammering in her chest. She felt as though she were falling slowly. She turned to Daniel, who gazed at her knowingly. "Danny," she said, completely flummoxed, "what just happened?"

He kissed her forehead. "Exactly what I predicted the night we left for Lowenstein's."

Just then she felt her phone vibrate. She pulled it out. A text from Ethan.

Meet me at the stage door in 30. Gotta let the crowd dissipate. Loved having you out there tonight.

Her hands shaking a little, she texted back.

See you in 30. You're a superstar.

§

Ethan found Max waiting on the couch in his dressing room with a dumbfounded look on his face.

"I can't believe you did that," he said once the backstage noise was shut out.

Ethan grinned sheepishly. "I didn't do anything."

"You sang her a love song, you dummy," Max said, and swatted his shoulder. "Your fans are going to be going insane. You're gonna break the internet. Again."

Unconcerned, Ethan changed out of his sweat-soaked shirt before chatting with the band for a few minutes. Despite his growing impatience, he thanked the venue staff and his back-up singers, and finally headed to the stage door, eager to see Evie.

CHAPTER SIXTEEN ♫

Ethan waited impatiently just inside the stage door for an answer to his text. The concert had lasted longer than he'd intended. He had bantered more than usual between songs, the extra energy coming from knowing that Evie was out there. Every moment he was onstage, he felt her presence. He hoped that the audience was eager to leave to pay babysitters or hang out in a bar so that he wouldn't walk into a mob clamoring for selfies. Tonight was not the night.

Had he gone too far?

His phone trilled. Evie.

Ten or so fans around. But you won't get mobbed or anything.

Ethan gestured to Max, who peeked out the door and looked left and right. He stepped back and said, "Nobody rabid. Just a few hopefuls."

Heart pounding, Ethan stepped outside. He could hear the traffic whizzing by on the street to the north, but the area behind the House of Blues was nearly empty. The small group of fans called to him and he waved as he walked over to them. While he took selfies and signed autographs, his apprehension increased. He felt his palms go clammy. After one final selfie, he said his goodbyes and turned to his friends.

The twin Marina Towers rose up behind Evie, Daniel, and Max. He shivered as he walked over, not sure if it was the chill in the air, or the expectation of meeting Evie's eyes.

Daniel got to him first and hugged him tightly. "You're a fucking rockstar, man. That was amazing."

"He's pretty talented," Evie said. Over Daniel's shoulder, he saw her standing with an expression on her face he couldn't read.

"Thank you." He let Daniel go and took a few steps over to her. To his surprise, she threw her arms around him.

"I can't believe you're mine, you talented, charming, ridiculous person."

He pulled back and gazed into her eyes. "I'm definitely yours."

Another unreadable expression flashed across her face.

"I'm all keyed up. Let's get a drink." Max grabbed Daniel's hand.

"Okay, yea, that sounds pretty good," Daniel said in an odd voice. He was clearly trying to play casual.

Evie pulled away from Ethan. She searched Daniel's face.

"What the fuck, Danny? What?"

Daniel's eyes filled with tears and his smile grew impossibly wider.

"Danny!" Evie shrieked, as if finally figuring it out.

He nodded and she leapt into his arms.

Ethan stepped back, wondering what this was all about.

"I'm going to Broadway, baby," Daniel said into her hair.

"Holy shit, dude, that is amazing." Ethan beamed, a million possibilities running through his mind. This news elated him.

As soon as Daniel set Evie down, Max threw his arms around Daniel's neck. He put his hands on either side of Daniel's face and kissed him.

Evie interrupted the kiss by throwing her arms around both Daniel and Max.

Ethan rushed to them and threw his arms around all three. They whooped and hollered, jumping together in a circle, making a scene. Gasping for breath, they separated.

Ethan put a hand on Daniel's shoulder. "You got the part."

Daniel nodded, seeming overcome. "I got the part."

"He got the part!" Max yelled.

"He got the part, Chicago!" Evie all but screamed, her arms spread wide and her head tilted to the sky.

Collapsing together in mirth, they began to walk toward the sidewalk arm in arm. Ethan felt his own eyes fill with tears. There was nothing like the triumph of getting something worked hard for. He knew how hard Daniel had had to work to get where he was going.

Evie suddenly gasped bringing them all to a halt. She smacked Daniel. "You are a liar," she accused him, laughing. "You knew before the show started."

Daniel nodded. "I couldn't tell you right before the concert. You wouldn't have been able to concentrate on this beautiful man. Plus, it felt nice just to sit with it for a while by myself."

"Oh my god, this is the best. Let's go to the bar." Evie was bouncing with excitement. She crashed into Ethan's side and he put his arm around her, nearly falling over. Brazenly, as he didn't see any more fans around, he pulled her closer and kissed her triumphantly.

They followed Max and Daniel to the street, where they waited for the cab. Ethan tried to be nonchalant but couldn't help overhearing their conversation.

"This means you're moving to New York, then," Max said.

"I suppose it does."

Ethan looked down at Evie, who also seemed to be pretending not to listen. She grinned.

"Then…I guess I should tell you that I can't stop thinking about you and I want to be with you."

Evie squeezed Ethan's hand, her face full of hope.

"I thought you'd never ask," Daniel said. He wrapped his arms around Max and they kissed until the cab pulled up to the curb.

"Oi, lovebirds," Ethan said. They broke apart, victory all over their faces. Ethan ushered them into the car.

Ethan put his arm around Evie, who sat in the middle of the backseat. Her voice was low when she murmured in his ear. "Hey, so, you sang me a love song, I'm pretty sure."

"Yeah, pretty sure I did that," he concurred.

"You wanna add, I dunno, some sort of disclaimer or something?"

He regarded her narrowed eyes and that sexy half smile. "Nope."

She snuggled closer to him.

"Hey, Ethan," Daniel said from the front seat. "What did you say you sing when you're feeling triumphant?"

"*Dreamgirls.*"

Ten minutes later, the foursome tumbled out of the cab, belting out "And I'm Telling You I'm Not Going" from the iconic musical. Ethan was sure that the cabbie was glad to see them go.

He bought the first round and Evie raised her glass.

"To my Danny. My love, my heart, my best guy. I have never been prouder of anyone than I am tonight. You are going to blow them all away."

Glasses were clinked and Ethan snaked his arm around Evie.

"To Chicago." He raised his glass at the boys.

"Chicago," they said in unison.

Evie looked into her drink for a moment, as if considering something. "To the future, and to endless possibilities."

Ethan met her eyes over their clinking glasses. He'd never seen such a bright green. They sparkled.

"To Max, and to me, and to our brand-new relationship," Daniel called over the table.

Ethan couldn't stop laughing. A joy blossomed inside him that he wasn't sure he'd felt before. For another hour, he felt a friendship cement between the four of them as they toasted to everything under the sun.

§

"I have a surprise," Evie said as they walked back to her condo.

"I love a surprise."

Inside, she pulled a cheesecake out of her refrigerator. "It's no Mrs. Carter's cheesecake, but it is from my favorite bakery." She pulled two forks out of a drawer.

He took a fork and followed her to the floor in front of the windows. "That was a very good night, that night," Ethan said. He recalled the night they met, the mystery of her, the almost desperation he felt for her to stay with him. He sat facing her, just as he had then.

"It was, wasn't it?"

He dug into the cheesecake. "Okay, it's not my mom's, but it is excellent."

"I'm glad you like it."

A peace settled around them. She licked her fork.

He set his down and moved the cheesecake aside, clearing his throat.

She looked at him expectantly.

"Evie," he began. He curled a strand of her hair around his finger.

"I'm just...gone. Just head over heels. And I want you to know. I'm all in. If you wanted to... I mean, I don't know exactly. Just... I need you to know that the ball is in your court. Because I'm in this, completely." He was stammering, but he didn't care.

Evie looked deep into his eyes. Time seemed to stop as she seemed to measure her words.

"Ethan, I don't have words for you now. But you have... You've been heard."

He nodded, a little disappointed but still optimistic. "I understand. I told you I was a bit much sometimes."

She chuckled. After a few more bites of cheesecake, they climbed into bed together. She could tell he was exhausted. He spooned her and she could feel his breathing grow even almost immediately. She felt so safe with him. Pulling his arm tighter around her, she thought through the evening's events. She felt a relief--she wasn't ready to hear the words she thought he wanted to say. And she wasn't sure yet that she knew how to love him. But then she thought of the love song, the toasts, Daniel's impending move to New York--what all of that could mean for her future, and if she was ready for it.

They spent much of Sunday in bed, making love, eating, and watching television. It was so easy to relax with him. Ethan fielded calls and emails from his people. Evie scanned Tumblr and Twitter mentions.

One photo from outside the House of Blues, capturing the moment Ethan hugged her and Max and Daniel, had to be her favorite invasion of privacy yet.

She took him to the airport Monday morning, where he kissed her so completely, she became weak in the knees.

"All in," he said, and kissed her nose. "See you soon, Freckles."

"See you soon, Carter." She watched him walk away, while thinking about everything she had been feeling since the night they met. The connection between them had been so unexpected. She felt tethered to Ethan in a way she had only ever felt with Liam. The pain of losing her husband and everything she had with him, she could feel it turning into something different. That pain would never go away, but she could see past it now, could feel it fading into something manageable.

Everything Ethan had said and done to make her feel safe and cared for raced through her mind.

§

Daniel needed an apartment, so the time between Evie's visits with Ethan was much shorter as she helped him look for one. A little over a week after the Chicago concert, she was back in New York. By day, they searched Manhattan, Brooklyn, and Queens for Daniel's perfect home. By night, Daniel hung out with Max or other friends, and Ethan and Evie wrapped themselves around each other again.

§

One day in mid-December Ethan didn't hear from Evie at all. The next day she seemed distant. When he asked her what was wrong, her response was vague. He couldn't figure it out, until he remembered the wedding photograph he'd seen in her dining room. A winter wedding.

He asked Daniel, who confirmed his suspicion. Her wedding anniversary had just passed, her second one without Liam.

He made a note of the date and let the subject go.

She didn't bring it up.

§

On another visit, just before Christmas, Daniel found the perfect place in Queens. He, Max, Evie, and Ethan all celebrated over dinner that evening.

Later, back in Ethan's apartment, they lay on the floor, contented, the lights from his Christmas tree twinkling above them. Her head was on his chest as he stroked her back. When Ethan sighed, she tilted her head to look at him.

He kissed her eyelashes and pulled her closer.

"So, Daniel is moving to New York," she said.

"What are you going to do without him?" he asked her.

Keel over and die, I expect, she heard Daniel say in her head. She stilled, quiet and contemplative. After a while she said, "It won't be easy living without him being a block and a half away. He's a part of me. He's family."

"You know..." Ethan hesitated, as if choosing his words carefully. "Brooklyn isn't terribly far from Queens."

She looked up at him, her eyes sending a warning that she was not ready to discuss it.

Ethan was a patient man. She hoped he knew she would arrive at the decision on her own. She took his hand, tracing his long fingers with her own. "You're a wonderful partner, Carter."

"You are, too. We're a good team."

She kissed him softly. She found it difficult to parse out her feelings when she was with him. In his arms, everything always felt perfect. But when they parted, she knew the doubts would come flooding back.

§

Between bouts of packing up Daniel's apartment, Evie and Daniel ice skated in Millennium Park, wandered the shops of the Magnificent Mile, and soaked up all that the Chicago holiday season had to offer before he left for a brand new life. Once he got to New York, he'd be stuck in rehearsal rooms all day. A fate, he admitted, for which he could not wait.

Ethan sent Evie a link to a promotional interview he'd done before a concert in Rhode Island.

I couldn't help it. You're so important to me.

She clicked the link. He'd finally answered the question about someone special in his life.

> The corners of his mouth pulled up.
> "Yeah, there is," Carter said bashfully.
> "And I won't say anything more about it,
> but she's incredibly special." As evidence,
> listen to him cover "If I Loved You"
> from Carousel this Saturday night. There
> is nothing sweeter than his voice in that
> song.

His social media mentions blew up again, of course, because his fans were nothing if not obsessive. It was the first time he'd confirmed a special person in his life since the stalking incident.

"Hey, Freckles," he said on Facetime one evening near New Year's Eve, "you're coming out to help Daniel get his new place set up, right?"

"Of course. And to see you."

"Excellent. Then I was thinking that I could come out to you sometime later in February."

"That would be great," she said, admiring his restraint. He hadn't brought up her moving to New York at all since the last night she'd seen him, as subtle as that was, though it weighed heavily on her mind.

"But..."

She cringed at his expression. "What is it?"

"After that it might get a little difficult. I just got a call," he said, and a huge grin spread across his face. "I got cast in a new series for Netflix, that one I auditioned for right after we met. We start filming in March, here in New York."

"Ethan. That is amazing. Congratulations."

He sobered. "The downside is, even if you come here, I won't have much time to spend with you. And I'm doing that Actor's Fund benefit concert too, so rehearsals are taking some time..."

"Carter."

"Yeah?"

"That's fucking amazing. I'm really proud of you, and I'm so excited for you, and we'll take it day by day, okay?"

"Filming a TV show is a lot, Evie. Twelve-hour days. For weeks sometimes. I'll have weekends, but I'll be exhausted," he said, as if trying to impress upon her how hard it was going to get.

"I understand that. So it'll be harder than it already is." She shrugged.

"It will."

"And it will be all that much sweeter when we get to see each other again," she said, and smiled.

His expression softened. "It will."

Evie's heart was still chained by events in the past and what she'd lost. Her fear of projecting what she'd felt for Liam onto Ethan was palpable. She didn't want to get serious with Ethan and then discover that her feelings for him were just because she missed her husband. But she couldn't help thinking maybe there was a time and place for them. She wanted to give in to her feelings, and she didn't want to rush herself. But she realized she might be running out of time. Ethan could easily move on.

§

The day of Daniel's final departure to New York, Evie sighed as she looked around his empty apartment. She had spent so many nights there: crying, laughing, getting drunk and silly, and scream-singing show tunes, much to the neighbors' chagrin.

Daniel curled an arm around her shoulder. "This is it," he said, as tears filled his eyes.

She began to cry in earnest. "I can't believe we're not going to be neighbors anymore."

They held each other tightly, and eventually Evie looked up at him. "Daniel. You are perfect and beautiful and the best human being on the planet. Broadway doesn't even know what's coming for them."

He bowed his head until their foreheads touched.

"I couldn't have asked for a better friend. You are a magical, hilarious piece of perfect, my little minx." They held each other a moment longer, holding ten years' worth of friendship wrapped around them. Finally, they wiped their eyes, walked outside to Evie's car, and headed to the airport.

They didn't speak on the way, just played songs they loved to sing together. As Evie pulled into the drop-off area, Daniel turned to her.

"Evelyn, I will only say this once more. You should come to New York with me. I know that means that you'd be completely removed from your old life and that's what's stopping you. I know you think for some reason that what you and Liam had will disappear if you leave that condo and truly move on. But that will never happen.

"Liam will always be with you. Leaving Chicago will not diminish what you had with him, not for a second." He took her hand and kissed it.

She closed her eyes. Not for the first time, Daniel understood her far better than she did herself.

Daniel pulled his luggage out and set it on the sidewalk before turning to her and opening his arms.

"Max is the luckiest guy in the world." She held onto him tightly.

He squeezed her back. "Think about what I said. I love you." He kissed her cheek and walked into the terminal.

As Evie drove home, her mind was racing.

§

Ethan hadn't brought up the fact that he wanted to be with Evie for real again, not once. He hadn't said he loved her, though he was full to bursting with it. He was trying to have patience because he didn't want to push her too fast. But even so, he was floundering a bit, unsure where to go from where they were. The good news about his career set him reeling in two directions: the joy of working steadily again and the inability to see Evie pretty much whenever he wanted. Nearly five months had passed since they'd met, and he was ready to start a life together with her, at the very least in the same city.

At his first rehearsal for the Actor's Fund benefit concert, he and Dion sang their duet. They took their notes from the director, sang it through once again, and then took a break in a corner of the studio.

Dion took a sip of water and capped the bottle. He planted his elbows on his knees and stared at Ethan.

Ethan arched a brow. "What?"

"Whatever happened to that redhead you were with at that party?" Dion said.

Ethan swigged from his water bottle, trying to remain nonchalant. "She's still around," he said.

"O-o-oh?"

Ethan regarded him for a moment, while half-listening to the other artists practice. His old friend scooted closer, an encouraging look on his face.

"This is just like being back in our dressing rooms eight shows a week. You being nosy."

"And you holding back all the time, except when onstage. Come on, man, you can talk to me. What's going on?"

Ethan sighed and began to speak quietly. "We met the night of the Lowenstein's concert. There was this immediate connection with her and I asked her out for a drink, and I learned..." He hesitated. He wanted to talk to someone about Evie, and he couldn't talk to Max. Though he trusted Max, it could still get to Daniel, who could tell her... He didn't want to risk it.

"Ethan, it's me."

He bumped his fist against Dion's. Of course he could trust him. "I learned that she's a widow. So we agreed that it was just going to be a fling. Just for the weekend, something fun and distracting. But man. I liked her. I really liked her. And we were both so sad when she left. Like, devastated. She came to New York again and I did the show in Chicago, and that night we found out that her best friend is going to move here. And she's visited a couple of times since.

"I have never been so comfortable, so happy with a woman. She's incredible."

"I really liked her."

"Yeah, she's... She's so understanding and fun and laid-back and hilarious--"

"You've got it bad."

"I do. I really do."

"I don't think I've ever heard you like this."

"And now, I don't know what to say to her," Ethan concluded. "I don't know how to tell her, without scaring her away or causing her pain, that I can't imagine life without her,"

Dion nodded. "So, you're in love with her."

Ethan hadn't used those words. He stared across the rehearsal studio and ran his hands over his face.

"I really-- Yeah, I am. I don't know if I've *ever* been so in love with someone." He glanced back at Dion.

To his surprise, Dion was grinning widely. "Does she know that?"

Ethan shook his head. "I don't think so. I've alluded to it, but I've never said it out loud."

"Well, what's the harm in telling her? Everyone wants to be loved. She should know. You make it sound like it's complicated and delicate, but dude. She should know you're in love with her. Even I can see that, even in the last five minutes."

"You think I should just, what? Call her up and tell her?"

"No, man, not over the phone. When is she here next?"

"She's coming in this week to help Daniel unpack." Ethan smiled at the thought.

Dion clapped him on the shoulder. "There you go. Tell her. Tell her, because if you don't, she won't have all the information she needs to make a decision. And I'll say this: Blake is the best thing to ever happen to me. When we went out that first night and we made out in that little booth-- Look, that could have been anyone. But I knew. I knew Blake was the one." He smiled nostalgically.

Ethan nodded again, contemplating all that had just transpired. "Thanks, man," he said.

Dion grinned back, obviously thrilled that his friend was in love.

§

After a day of unpacking with Daniel in his new apartment, Ethan and Evie arrived back at his condo, exhausted. Ethan kept looking at Evie deeply, searching her face. Something was up with him.

"*Why* do you keep looking at me like that?" she finally said, after greeting Henry.

He just looked down into her eyes and shook his head. "You're just the most incredible human being, that's all."

She wrapped her arms around his waist. "Hey, likewise, Carter. You helped a practical stranger move. That's saint-like."

"I think it's safe to say that Daniel and I are friends now. You're the one who flew all the way here to help someone move."

"He's my Daniel." Up on her tiptoes, she found his lips with hers. "Shower?"

His lips stayed on hers as they moved into the bedroom. "Definitely."

She stayed in New York for a week, their longest stretch together. Their lives became choreography, and their days danced around each other. While he spent his evenings reviewing the pilot script he was about to film, she would make them dinner, and then go out to see Daniel. He went to the gym while she took her long walks. He got used to having her in his apartment when he got home from rehearsals, meetings, and costume fittings, began to look forward to the smell of food wafting out the door as he opened it.

The smiles she gave him after only hours apart thrilled him to his bones. She once confessed she was surprised at how comfortable she felt, being in his life for such a long stretch, how at home in his apartment.

Since the Rhode Island piece, his fans seemed to accept that there was someone in his life. Nothing frightening was occurring online, and because of that, he took her to a couple of musicals. Her excitement when he took her backstage to meet the casts melted his heart.

He was enamored with the passion she had for changing the world for the better, thrilled that they had the same desire for social justice. She shared his view that live theatre made the world a better place, and mentioned she missed working for the non-profit.

Toward the end of the week, he gave her a list of theatre education focused non-profits in New York. But that's as far as he got to asking her to move there.

He didn't say he loved her.

Every time he tried, fear would pull him back. She could just get up and leave if she felt too much pressure, and that was the last thing he wanted. Even so, his resistance was starting to wane, and he knew he wouldn't be able to keep it in much longer.

The week came to a close much too quickly. She and Ethan stood at the airport once again, looking deeply into each other's eyes. Now was the time to tell her he was in love with her.

Ethan took a deep breath.

"Evie," he said, while tucking a strand of hair behind her ear.

Her eyes filled with tears and he stopped. He remembered that she was also saying goodbye to Daniel, going back to her life in Chicago without him. He could see she was struggling. It was as if her head and her heart were at odds. He wasn't sure if telling her would add to the confusion he knew she was feeling or ease it. He couldn't do it. He knew it would be too much at that moment.

Evie rose up and kissed him intensely, as if trying to convey everything she was feeling through this one kiss.

"I'll call you when I get off the plane," she said, and she walked away quickly.

He watched her go, a pain knifing through his heart.

Dion was right. He regretted not telling her the moment she walked away, but he couldn't add to the hurt in her eyes.

Even worse, they hadn't made plans to see each other again, not knowing exactly what Ethan's schedule would be.

He got in his car and drove home, frustrated and sad and loving her.

CHAPTER SEVENTEEN ♫

Evie stepped into her condo and dropped her bag at her feet. Leaning against the door, she felt an emptiness, a palpable loss. Daniel was no longer down the street. She wandered around, picking things up and putting them down again, the too familiar rooms feeling suddenly foreign. Without Liam, without Daniel…without Ethan, her home felt suddenly cold. She opened the patio door and walked out. The chill of Chicago winter washed over her. The tears were cold on her face and she let them come. For a long time, she stood, gazing at the city lights and the sliver of Lake Michigan she could see through the buildings to the east.

She ran the sleeves of her coat over her face and with nearly numb fingers, she Facetimed Ethan.

His smile faded almost immediately when he saw her face. She was sure it was clear that she'd been crying. "Hey, Freckles," he said. His voice was full of concern.

She attempted a grin but knew it was shaky. "Hey. I miss you already." Her words caught in her throat.

Taking a deep breath, he looked away, seeming to choose his words carefully. "I miss you, too. I don't even have words for how badly I wish you were with me right now. And Evie… I…"

She inhaled unsteadily and waited. If he said the words, if he said he loved her, she would know what to do. Wouldn't she?

"I'm here. I'm right here."

She let go of the breath she didn't know she was holding. "I know. I do."

"Okay."

He asked about her flight and attempted small talk, but the tension in her chest mounted and she told him she needed to unpack. He sounded dejected when they said goodbye.

Now chilled to the bone, she stepped inside. Why didn't he tell her? Had she misinterpreted everything? Were the intense feelings she had for Ethan just a projection? Did he love her?

She pulled her phone out again and scrolled through the photos they'd taken together on their visits. Goofy selfies with pulled faces, Ethan and Henry, his arms wrapped around her, his beautiful smile.

Her mind was spinning, the questions swirling around, the indecision tying her in knots.

Closing her eyes, she raised her hand to touch her and Liam's wedding rings. She remembered the day she returned from Italy and had taken his ring out of her bag. Lovingly, she had threaded it on a chain and hung it around her neck. She didn't take it off. Not for a year.

On the anniversary of his death, she had removed her gold band and strung it next to Liam's. It was her first attempt to move on.

Now, she found she needed the comfort the rings had always given her.

They weren't there.

Feeling short of breath, she remembered when she took them off. Not wanting to lose the rings in all the traveling she'd been doing, she had tucked them safely in a drawer before her third visit to New York.

In a sudden, blinding rush, she felt clarity.

She dialed her realtor.

§

Ethan stepped into his apartment, void again of Evie's presence. He tossed his bag onto a chair and collapsed onto the couch. The script he was supposed to be memorizing seemed to taunt him from the coffee table. He scowled at it, then got up and began pacing the room.

He was more sure that Evie was his forever than he had been about anything in his life. So why couldn't he just say it? It was easy to find an excuse--it was terrifying to put her in the public eye. He didn't want to add to her sadness or confusion--it was terrifying to tell a person you loved them. But wasn't his whole job about being vulnerable? About stripping down and finding the truth? Why couldn't he translate that to his life?

He groaned aloud, angry with himself. Out on the balcony, he watched a plane fly over the river. Maybe it was Evie's. He closed his eyes, willing her to feel his heart.

A week later, though Ethan was still mentally kicking himself, he felt a satisfying rush being back on set. He was thrilled to be back to work--emotional, grueling work--and glad for the distraction from Evie. They still communicated all the time, but something was strained. She seemed distant and he was at a loss.

While pacing his trailer on his last day of filming for the week, he got a text from her.

Hey, where are you today, time to talk?

His heart nearly stopped. This was it then, she was going to break it off, he was sure of it.

At the studio, supposed to be here til two.
So that means five. Call you then?

Sure.

Sure. That was it. One word.

He threw his phone onto the couch and raked his hands through his hair. He resumed his frantic pacing, practically wringing his hands. At the small mirror near the trailer door, he caught his own reflection. He stared at his troubled face.

"No," he said aloud. "It's not ending like this. No way." He retrieved his phone.

Despite the cold, there was a significant gathering of fans around the studio entrance as Ethan emerged that evening. *Dammit.* In his haste, he'd forgotten to take the back way out. The fans were there mostly for the actor playing Ethan's younger brother, who had a huge following thanks to a recent blockbuster he'd been in. The security guard had even put the ropes and stanchions out tonight to keep them from getting out of hand.

Ethan didn't love facing a crowd after a long day of work, but he still paused for a few selfies and autographs. His name was called several times, but there was so much noise, he couldn't see where it was coming from. He was finding it hard to hide his impatience as more fans clamored for a photo.

Looking down at his watch, he started. He was going to have to rush to catch his flight.

He really felt like this was a romantic comedy now.

Or a tragedy. Depending on how tonight went.

Finally, he broke free of the autograph-seekers and said, "Thanks, you guys, but I have a flight to catch." He waved and turned towards the line of waiting town cars.

"Oh my *god.*"

He stopped short.

"Carter, you idiot, turn around. Do you really want to get on that plane?"

He turned slowly, hope blossoming in his chest, and stood where he was, rooted to the spot.

Evie fought her way through the fans and stood at the front of the rope line.

Finally.

"Oh, thank god," he said, unable to move.

"I…took a redeye last night. Thought I'd try my hand at romance. I didn't expect…uh…" She gestured to the people surrounding her.

Ethan's castmates and the fans all seemed to understand something big was happening and were watching this scene play out intently.

He shook his head, her presence in front of him sinking in. A chuckle escaped him. "I bought a ticket to Chicago this morning," he finally said.

She laughed. "Don't sell your pocket watch."

"Don't sell your hair," he replied, loving that he understood her reference. He could feel an impossibly wide grin grow across his face, and her smile was the brightest he'd ever seen. The security guard, clearly sensing it was the right time, pulled the rope high enough for Evie to get under.

Ethan took a deep breath as she came slowly toward him. When she stopped, he took her hand and placed it on his heart.

"I am absolutely, irrevocably in love with you, Evie." Relief and nervousness flooded through him. "I don't want to spend another second without you."

She stood in front of him, that steely gaze he knew so well and loved so fiercely meeting his.

"Good," she said, "because I put the condo on the market a week ago and I did my last shift at the shelter yesterday." She stepped closer, until their bodies fit together perfectly. "I'm all in, Carter. I love you, completely. Will you spend your life with me?"

He pulled her close, and their lips met. He felt the last piece of a puzzle slide into place.

They drew apart and got into the waiting car.

EPILOGUE ♫

Five Years Later

"And the American Theatre Wing Tony Award goes to...Ethan Carter!"

The audience roared, joy at Ethan finally getting a Tony filling Radio City Music Hall. Overcome, Ethan buried his face in his hands for several moments. He wiped his eyes and stood, then pulled a beaming Evie to him and kissed her.

Her heart was bursting with pride and she gave him a small shove toward the stage. "Go get 'em, tiger," she whispered.

He kissed her again and strode to the stage. On the way, Dion clapped him on the back and both Daniel and Max caught him in a brief hug. Evie looked on with pleasure as Ethan accepted his statue and stepped up to the mic.

The amber lighting shone down from the domed ceiling of the hall, shedding a warm light on Broadway's best talent. Evie looked around at the people she now knew and loved, all dressed to the nines. She couldn't quite believe this was her life. Ethan stood on the vast, ornate stage looking like a rock star in his slim-cut maroon tuxedo.

"I've always said that awards aren't the reason to do the work, but I am so honored by this. Thank you. I'm just..." He ran his hands through his hair, as if searching for the right words. She knew he hadn't prepared a speech, afraid that doing so would jinx his chances. He thanked his cast and crew before looking toward Evie.

She put a hand over her heart and smiled, mouthing 'I love you'.

"And you. Evie. My partner. You are the most hilarious, fearless nerd I have ever known. Sharing my life with you is the best thing that ever happened to me, and I don't need this award to know that--" His voice caught. "--I am the luckiest man in the world."

The audience began to applaud, and he grinned down at the statue in his hand. "It, uh, it is pretty great though. Thank you!" He raised the Tony in triumph and received a standing ovation.

Backstage, Evie held him tightly for a long time. She had seen the sacrifices he had made for the taxing role which had won him the award and could think of no one more deserving.

The rest of the evening was a whirlwind of glittering parties and congratulations. They danced and laughed and drank until they stumbled into their condo in the wee hours of the morning. They collapsed on the bed, exhausted. Ethan leaned back against the headboard and cradled the Tony in his hands. She had never seen him look so happy.

Evie curled into him and pulled his tie off. She twirled the little disc in the Tony. "What next, Carter?"

"Who knows?" He looked straight into her eyes. "Will you be there?"

"Always."

"Then I don't need to know anything else, Freckles."

About the Author

With over ten years of wedding planning experience and a lifetime onstage, Avery Easton knows romance. When she was seven years old, in a pink Snoopy notebook, she began writing stories, and hasn't stopped since. If she's not reading or writing, you can find her cross stitching or belting out showtunes. She lives in Chicago with her husband and two adorable cats. Follow her on Instagram @averyeastonwrites.

If you would like to make a donation to Broadway Cares / Equity Fights AIDS, please visit BroadwayCares.org.

Love Me A Little is also available in eBook by Uncial Press, an imprint of GCT, Inc. Visit us at uncialpress.com

Made in the USA
Monee, IL
28 September 2020